What Kids Say About
Carole Marsh Mysteries . . .

"I love the real locations! Reading the book always makes me want to go and visit them all on our next family vacation. My mom says maybe, but I can't wait!"

"One day, I want to be a real kid in one of Ms. Marsh's mystery books. I think it would be fun, and I think I am a real character anyway. I filled out the application and sent it in and am keeping my fingers crossed!"

"History was not my favorite subject until I started reading Carole Marsh Mysteries. Ms. Marsh really brings history to life. Also, she leaves room for the scary and fun. "

"I think Christina is so smart and brave. She is lucky to be in the mystery books because she gets to go to a lot of places. I always wonder just how much of the book is true and what is made up. Trying to figure that out is fun!"

"Grant is cool and funny! He makes me laugh a lot!"

"I like that there are boys and girls in the story of different ages. Some mysteries I outgrow, but I can always find a favorite character to identify with in these books."

"They are scary, but not too scary. They are funny. I learn a lot. There is always food which makes me hungry. I feel like I am there."

What Parents and Teachers Say about Carole Marsh Mysteries . . .

"I think kids love these books because they have such a wealth of detail. I know I learn a lot reading them! It's an engaging way to look at the history of any place or event. I always say I'm only going to read one chapter to the kids, but that never happens—it's always two or three, at least!"
—Librarian

"Reading the mystery and going on the field trip—Scavenger Hunt in hand—was the most fun our class ever had! It really brought the place and its history to life. They loved the real kids characters and all the humor. I loved seeing them learn that reading is an experience to enjoy!"
—4th grade teacher

"Carole Marsh is really on to something with these unique mysteries. They are so clever; kids want to read them all. The Teacher's Guides are chock full of activities, recipes, and additional fascinating information. My kids thought I was an expert on the subject—and with this tool, I felt like it!"
—3rd grade teacher

"My students loved writing their own Real Kids/Real Places mystery book! Ms. Marsh's reproducible guidelines are a real jewel. They learned about copyright and more & ended up with their own book they were so proud of!"
—Reading/Writing Teacher

"The kids seem very realistic—my children seemed to relate to the characters. Also, it is educational by expanding their knowledge about the famous places in the books."

"They are what children like: mysteries and adventures with children they can relate to."

"Encourages reading for pleasure."

"This series is great. It can be used for reluctant readers, and as a history supplement."

The Mystery of the HAUNTED GHOST TOWN

CAROLE MARSH MYSTERIES™

by
Carole Marsh

Published by Gallopade International/Carole Marsh Books. Printed in the United States of
America.

Managing Editor: Sherry Moss
Senior Editor: Janice Baker
Assistant Editor: Fran Kramer
Cover Design: Vicki DeJoy
Cover Photo Credits: Eric Hood, istockphoto, ©Jupiterimages Corporation
Picture Credits: Vicki DeJoy
Content Design and Illustrations: Randolyn Friedlander

Gallopade International is introducing SAT words that kids need to know in each new book
that we publish. The SAT words are bold in the story. Look for this special logo **SAT**
beside each word in the glossary. Happy Learning!

Gallopade is proud to be a member and supporter of these educational organizations and
associations:

American Booksellers Association
American Library Association
International Reading Association
National Association for Gifted Children
The National School Supply and Equipment Association
The National Council for the Social Studies
Museum Store Association
Association of Partners for Public Lands
Association of Booksellers for Children

30 YEARS AGO . . .

As a mother and an author, one of the fondest periods of my life was when I decided to write mystery books for children. At this time (1979) kids were pretty much glued to the TV, something parents and teachers complained about the same way they do about web surfing and video games today.

I decided to set each mystery in a real place—a place kids could go and visit for themselves after reading the book. And I also used real children as characters. Usually a couple of my own children served as characters, and I had no trouble recruiting kids from the book's location to also be characters.

Also, I wanted all the kids—boys and girls of all ages—to participate in solving the mystery. And, I wanted kids to learn something as they read. Something about the history of the location. And, I wanted the stories to be funny. That formula of real+scary+smart+fun served me well.

I love getting letters from teachers and parents who say they read the book with their class or child, then visited the historic site and saw all the places in the mystery for themselves. What's so great about that? What's great is that you and your children have an experience that bonds you together forever. Something you shared. Something you both cared about at the time. Something that crossed all age levels—a good story, a good scare, a good laugh!

30 years later,

Carole Marsh

Hey, kids! As you see—here we are ready to embark on another of our exciting Carole Marsh Mystery adventures! You know, in "real life," I keep very close tabs on Christina, Grant, and their friends when we travel. However, in the mystery books, they always seem to slip away from Papa and me so they can try to solve the mystery on their own!

I hope you will go to www.carolemarshmysteries.com and apply to be a character in a future mystery book! Well, The *Mystery Girl* is all tuned up and ready for "take-off!"

Gotta go...Papa says so! Wonder what I've forgotten this time?

Happy "Armchair Travel" Reading,

Mimi

Christina Yother   **Grant Yother**   **Elijah Joiner**   **Erin Joiner**

ABOUT THE CHARACTERS

Christina Yother, 10, from Peachtree City, Georgia

Grant Yother, 7, from Peachtree City, Georgia, Christina's brother

Elijah Joiner, 6, from Peachtree City, Georgia, as Jorge

Erin Joiner, 8, from Peachtree City, Georgia, as Rosita

The many places featured in the book actually exist and are worth a visit! Perhaps you could read the book and follow the trail these kids went on during their mysterious adventure!

Titles in the Carole Marsh Mysteries Series

Books and Teacher's Guides are available at booksellers, libraries, school supply stores, museums, and many other locations!

CONTENTS

1 Biting the Dust

"Ghost towns! Are we going to see real ghost towns?" Grant asked his grandfather, Papa. "And REAL ghosts in the ghost towns?"

"Could be," replied Papa, as he checked the gages of his little red and white airplane, the *Mystery Girl*, preparing the plane for landing.

"Grant, there ARE no ghosts in ghost towns!" his sister, Christina, claimed in an older-sister, bossy way, as she tugged one of his blond curls. "I told you that! Papa, you're just leading Grant on!"

"Don't be too sure about that, Christina," Papa answered, with a twinkle in his eye. "I've been in ghost towns, and I'd swear I came across a ghost or two! Those towns just might be haunted." He laughed and added, "You'll see for yourself!"

"You'll have to make a believer out of me!" Christina declared, her arms thrust across her chest. She thought visiting ghost towns would be exciting, but certainly not scary. Sitting silently, her finger twirling a lock of her brown hair and her tongue toying with the

1

braces on her teeth, Christina wondered if Papa was right. She suspected he would tease her in some ghost town, probably acting like a ghost to scare her, just to prove his point. I'll have to keep an eye on him, Christina thought.

Christina and Grant often traveled with their grandparents. Their grandmother, Mimi, wrote mysteries for children, and often needed to do research in fascinating locations around the world. This trip, however, was a vacation. "There are no mysteries on my agenda, thank you very much!" Mimi had said when she invited the kids to come along.

Papa knew a lot about the Old West, and was something of a cowboy, always wearing jeans, a cowboy hat, and cowboy boots. With his stories of the Old West, Papa had no trouble convincing the kids to take this vacation in southern Arizona. They had looked forward to this trip for a long time, and now the day had finally come!

Mimi was not as thrilled. There was all that heat! And sun! And dust! She loved wearing hats and sparkly red sunglasses, and now had a good reason to wear them both—to protect her blond hair and fair skin from the blazing sun!

What Mimi did love was the scenery of the West. The stark desert, with its prickly cacti and multi-colored sunsets, stole her heart every time she saw it. Plus, she couldn't wait to get her hands on the stunning pieces of jewelry handcrafted by the Native Americans!

The *Mystery Girl* slowly descended to land at a local airport near Tombstone, Arizona. The plane was now low enough so the kids could see details on the ground below.

Christina gazed out the window on her side of the plane. Immediately below, there was nothing but dry and dusty yellow land, covered in spots by some low, drab shrub brush. Here and there, tumbleweeds lazily drifted in the sandy soil.

Grant's blue eyes popped open wide. "Is that Boot Hill Cemetery over there?" he yelled, jabbing his finger against the window on his side of the plane.

"Sure is," Papa said. "That's the real thing!"

"Wow—that's where the gunslingers are buried! Can we go there, Papa?" Grant asked, jumping up and down in his seat despite being **constrained** by his seat belt.

"It's just a bunch of tombstones," Christina remarked. She thought her little brother was silly to get so excited over an old cemetery. "You can see tombstones anywhere."

"Not like these," Papa said, with another of those twinkles in his eye. "You'll see!"

"OK, Papa...I suppose ghosts pop out from behind the tombstones and talk to you," Christina said. "Can't wait to see that!" She glanced out the window again to see a cloud of dust envelop the plane. Pebbles from the dirt runway rocketed everywhere, pelting the plane as it touched down.

Ping   PING   **POP**

Against the backdrop of the coffee-colored soil, Christina spotted a dark brown steer struggling to stand. Each time it got up, the bull collapsed again in a cloud of dust. The animal's legs were too weak for it to stand. A flock of buzzards slowly circled overhead.

Christina couldn't imagine a more **desolate** scene. She felt goose bumps on her neck. Maybe it wasn't just the ghost towns that were haunted, she thought. Maybe the whole place was haunted!

Little did she know how scary things could get in a ghost town—and a cemetery! This steer in distress was just the beginning of an Old West mystery!

2 Food for Thought

Soon after landing, Papa rented a red SUV (Mimi chose the color, of course!) for their vacation transportation.

"What should we do first?" Papa asked.

"Let's eat!" Grant cried. "My tummy is emptier than Mimi's swimming pool in January!"

"That's pretty empty," Papa replied. "Let's head this way."

Papa wheeled the SUV to a town outside Tombstone called Sunshine Gap. It was a small, dusty town with a few stores, a bank, a post office, a pizza parlor, and a restaurant. A big red and white sign advertised the eatery as the Lazy H Diner, a family restaurant with Western-style cooking.

Mimi leaned out of the SUV window and asked a local cowboy ambling along the sidewalk if the Lazy H Diner served good food.

"Yes, it does," he said, picking his teeth with a weed. "China Betty sets out the best vittles anywhere in these parts. All the locals like to chow down at China Betty's."

"China Betty's?" Mimi asked.

"Betty's Chinese place," the cowboy replied. "Her folks have been here from way back. They came to these parts to work on the railroad. She's had the Lazy H Diner most of forty years. 'Cept we don't call it the Lazy H. We call it China Betty's."

Mimi and Papa thanked the cowboy. Everyone decided that the Lazy H Diner, or China Betty's, would be a great place to eat. They stepped inside the cool, sunny diner to find it filled, not with tourists, but with local folks from Sunshine Gap.

"The food's got to be good," Papa said, eyeing a sizzling ribeye steak on someone's plate, "if the local people like to eat here."

A plump, young waitress, with a pencil thrust behind her ear and "Sally" on her nametag, seated the group at a booth near a window. Grant, curious to see a Chinese person in the Wild West, asked the waitress, "Is there REALLY a China Betty?"

"Sure is!" Sally replied. Then she yelled, "Hey, Betty! A little feller, no taller than knee-high to a grasshopper, wants to see you!"

The door to the kitchen swung open and a tiny, elderly Chinese lady stuck her head out and waved.

Capped gold teeth gleamed from a smile as wide as Texas. Grant waved back with a spoon in his hand.

The waitress looked back at her guests. Taking the pencil from behind her ear, she asked, "Now, what can I get you folks?"

Grant looked puzzled. "What are 'vittles'? If they're good, I'd like some."

The waitress laughed and said, "I can tell you're not from around here. Vittles is food. We got plenty of good vittles, thanks to China Betty."

"No wonder the local people like to eat here," Mimi said. "The food looks tasty and China Betty sure looks friendly. What looks good to everyone?"

"Ribs!" Grant yelled as he pointed to the top of the menu. "Mimi, they have barbequed ribs."

"The ribs are today's special," Sally said, jotting Grant's order on her pad.

Everyone else thought the ribs, along with fresh corn, coleslaw, and fries sounded good too. Before long, all table conversation ceased as Christina, Grant, Papa, and Mimi concentrated on eating their mouthwatering Western meal.

Christina was stuffing her last crispy french fry into her mouth when she overheard a loud, angry voice in the booth behind her.

"Two more of my cattle are sick," a man with scraggly red hair complained to his companion.

"That's a real shame, Big Jim," the friend answered. "A real shame."

Christina suddenly remembered the steer she saw from the airplane. Was that steer sick just like this man's cattle? What was happening?

3 Cattle Skedaddle!

Because everyone else in the restaurant also heard Big Jim, all conversation stopped with the mention of sick cattle. Even China Betty came out from the kitchen to hear what was happening. A Mexican man, sitting at a nearby table with his wife and kids, looked up. "You too, Big Jim?" he said. "Counting my sick cow, that makes three animals this week."

A wrinkled old man across the aisle said, "It ain't natural for so many livestock to get sick."

"I wonder if it's the water," Big Jim observed. "Maybe somethin's wrong with the water. It's not the food. I feed my cattle only the best."

"*Si*," the Mexican man said. "I think it's the water too. I had a health inspector check my well water. He said it didn't look right. He took some samples to test in his lab. He also said that if the water is polluted, it will require a major cleanup."

9

"Manuel," Big Jim remarked, "if you have bad water, and I do, many more probably do too. That's a problem for the whole town! Not only could our cattle get sick and die, but nobody will want to live here. Who wants to live in a polluted town?"

Manuel replied, "*Si*, and none of us can afford to pay for a major cleanup!"

A bearded man wearing a yellow bandana lifted up a glass of water and called out, "China Betty, what're you serving us to drink? Not bad water, I hope!"

"No such thing, Andy," China Betty said. "I buy my water! You all best buy yours in a store—or right here," she said, pointing to a refrigerator full of bottled water at the back of the restaurant.

Everyone let out a huge sigh of relief, glad to know the water they just drank for lunch didn't come from the old well behind the restaurant.

Big Jim said, "I was thinkin' of selling 40 acres. But with cattle dying, I don't know who'd buy the land. In fact, it would make any thinkin' man want to skedaddle!"

Grant leaned over to his grandfather. "Papa, what does a ski paddle have to do with cattle?" he asked. "Actually, what is a ski paddle?"

Papa smiled and said, "He didn't say, 'ski paddle.' The word is 'skedaddle.' It means to get out, or pick up and leave."

Grant said loudly, so everyone could hear, "It sounds like the cattle better skedaddle!"

Everyone laughed. Then Manuel said, "We can't leave and neither can our cattle, young man. We live here. This is our home. China Betty's family has lived here for 100 years or more." Manuel glanced at the frightened faces of his wife and kids. Sighing, he said, "We must find out what's happening and fix it."

China Betty nodded in agreement. "This town is so small," she said, "if just a few families leave, Sunshine Gap could become one more ghost town like so many others in Arizona—a pile of rubble and some cattle bones!"

4 Wakin' Snakes

Christina and Grant nibbled on ears of crisp yellow corn as they listened to the talk in the restaurant. Christina was very observant and liked to "people-watch." Here's a good chance to see the many types of people who live in Sunshine Gap, she thought. Like the famous detective Sherlock Holmes, Christina loved to guess about people's lives.

"I'll bet those two bow-legged guys are real cowboys," she whispered to Grant, using her piece of butter-drenched corn to point out two men in faded jeans. "Look at their spurs and boots," she added.

"Yep," Grant answered, with yellow bits of corn decorating his cheeks, "they seem to be really worried about their horses drinking the water."

"And that older man with the slicked-back hair and blue suit," Christina continued, "I bet he owns the bank because he's talking about money being hard to get."

"Look at that **CREEPY** guy sitting in the seat next to the banker," Grant said. "His eyelids don't blink much."

"Maybe that's why the other guys are calling him 'Dead Eye'," Christina observed. "He has a deadpan expression, hardly showing any emotion. With that poker face, do you suppose he's a gambler? I wonder what he does."

Dead Eye, at that very moment, answered Christina's question. He told the group he had sick cattle on his ranch too. So he's a rancher like just about everyone else, she thought.

Manuel leaned over to put his arm around the brown-eyed little girl next to him. "It isn't just that the cattle are sick," he said. "Our families are also affected, even if we drink water from a bottle!"

The little girl twisted her soft black braids of hair between her fingers. In a soft voice that made everyone strain to hear, she said, "Daddy, my little calf won't get sick, will it?"

Sitting next to the girl, a boy with thick bushy hair added, "And my colt?"

"No, my children," Manuel answered. "I'm digging a new well. Hopefully, it will have fresh, clean water."

Christina noticed two men sitting together in the corner, quietly sipping their coffee. One was tall, with brown hair and a rose tattoo on his upper left arm. The other was a Native American wearing a beaded necklace. Christina noticed their leather jackets, gloves, and helmets spread on the table and felt sure they rode the motorcycles she saw parked outside. She wondered why they didn't say anything. Maybe they were drifters, just passing through, she thought.

Just then, Big Jim said to the motorcycle rider with the tattoo, "Dusty, have you seen sick animals on other ranches when you bike through the hills?"

Dusty jumped at being spoken to so abruptly. "No, Big Jim," Dusty replied. He pointed to the man next to him. "My partner here, Navaho Joe, and I just see the usual. No sick cattle—just old buzzards flying over anything they can find."

Was it the water making the animals sick, or was it something else? Christina, ever the sleuth, wondered why the town was having this problem. She decided to share what she had seen when her family arrived on the *Mystery Girl.*

Christina rubbed her finger over her braces to make sure no corn was stuck there. "Mr. Big Jim," she said, not knowing what Big Jim's last name was, "this morning, I saw a bull that looked sick. It was near the small airport where we landed."

"Well, howdy to you, young lady," Big Jim said, turning in Christina's direction. "Don't believe we've met. I'm Jim Wilcox. People here just call me Big Jim." Big Jim stood up and came over to shake her hand. Christina could see in a moment why he was called Big

Jim—he was well over six feet tall with massive shoulders. His huge hand was like the paw of a bear.

"I'm Christina," she said, and then introduced Grant, Mimi, and Papa to Big Jim.

"What brings you to these parts?" Big Jim asked.

"We want to see ghosts in ghost towns!" Grant piped up.

"Well, sonny," Big Jim said, patting Grant on the head, "we've got plenty of ghosts and ghost towns. You've come to the right place. I bet you'll see all sorts of strange things."

Christina said, "I think it's odd that your cattle are getting sick. Do you really know why? Is it the water?"

"It appears we need to do something about this," Big Jim said, not answering her question directly.

The man who looked like a banker then prodded Big Jim, "You better do something about it soon if you want to keep being sheriff of this town."

Christina persisted with her question to Big Jim. "Has only Mr. Manuel tested his well water? Maybe everybody should get their water tested. If you know what's causing the problem, you'll know how to fix it."

"That's a good idea, young lady," Big Jim said, rubbing his chin.

Grant stood up in his chair. In a serious voice and standing tall, he addressed everyone in the restaurant. "I KNOW what's causing the animals to get sick!" Grant exclaimed. "IT'S THE GHOSTS!"

Everyone chuckled, looking at each other.

"That's as good a cause as any, sonny," Big Jim said, shaking his head. "Who knows what we will find when we start looking? It could be a snake pit of a problem."

From somewhere in the restaurant, a low voice muttered, "Maybe we should quit our yammerin', and don't go wakin' snakes."

There was complete silence in the restaurant. A few people stood up and left. Papa paid the bill, and Mimi and the kids walked to the parking lot outside the Lazy H Diner. While climbing into the SUV, Grant spotted something drawn in the dust on the back of their vehicle.

"Christina, what's this?" Grant asked, pointing to the scribbled drawing.

"It looks like a strange animal," Christina remarked, squinting to see in the bright sunlight.

"Oh, for goodness sake, wipe it off," Mimi said. "It gives me the creeps."

"Let me copy it first," Christina replied, pulling a piece of paper out of her notebook. "I want to find out what it means!"

With all the strange happenings in this town, a scary animal drawn on the back of their SUV must mean something, Christina thought. *And why did that voice in the restaurant warn against "waking snakes?" Was someone trying to scare people? And if so, why? Christina was sure no ghost drew this picture in broad daylight!*

5 Scared Like the Dickens

When everyone was settled in the SUV, Papa asked, "How about seeing Wyatt Earp and Doc Holliday shoot it out with the Clanton gang?"

"A real shoot 'em up gunfight?" Grant yelled, as he put his hands on his hips and pointed his fingers to imitate a gunslinger firing two pistols at the same time.

"Yep," Papa said, "a real shootout at the OK Corral, but without real bullets."

"COOOL!"

Grant squealed as he clapped his hands. "Where is it?"

"In Tombstone!" Papa said. "That's a good name for the site of a gunfight, don't you think?"

"How did the town get an awful name like that?" Christina asked, buckling her seat belt.

19

"The town's founder, a man named Ed Schieffelin, was told that he would only find his tombstone if he went looking for silver in this area," Papa replied. "He did find silver, which brought many other prospectors here. A town grew up, and Mr. Schieffelin thought Tombstone would be a good name for it."

As the SUV rolled into Tombstone, Christina thought the town looked like a cleaned-up version of its real past. There were ancient-looking wood and adobe buildings lining the sides of the street. The old court house was one of the few brick structures. Horses were even tied up in front of a few buildings, their bushy tails swatting at pesky flies.

After Papa parked the SUV, the group decided to take a stroll along the main street. They followed a group of tourists to the OK Corral, a tan adobe building with a lot in the back. Papa bought tickets for the next shootout performance, and the kids slithered up front for a good spot to watch the gunfight.

The crowd hushed as four men packing pistols warily patrolled the street.

Papa whispered, "That's Doc Holliday and the Earp Brothers, Wyatt, Virgil, and Morgan. They're trying to keep the peace and keep armed cowboys out of the town."

From the other end of the street, five more cowboys meandered out. Papa again explained, "That's Ike and

Billy Clanton, the McLaury brothers, and Billy Claiborne. They are cowboys who have had their differences with the Earps. A few of the cowboys have broken the rule about having guns in town. Watch them—they're armed!"

Grant covered his ears and closed his eyes at the deafening racket of the mock shootout. When he opened them, the "dead" men were lying on the ground, and the wounded ones were stumbling away.

"Who really got killed?" Grant asked.

"The cowboys, Billy Clanton and the two McLaury brothers," Papa said. "Would you like to see where the real cowboys are buried?"

"Sure! Are they buried in Boot Hill?" Grant asked, his blue eyes wide with anticipation.

"Yep," Papa answered. "It's not far from here."

"Do you think their ghosts are in the cemetery?" Grant wanted to know.

"Could well be," Papa said, smiling. "But I don't think they will hurt anyone."

"In THAT case," Grant replied, "let's go!"

Papa drove the kids and Mimi to Boot Hill, a dusty, rocky hill located outside of town. "Here we are," Papa announced. "Boot Hill Graveyard, founded in 1878."

"Wow, it's kind of spooky-looking," Christina said. "It's so dreary!"

"Why do they call it 'Boot Hill'?" Grant asked. "I don't see any boots, except on Papa's feet!"

Mimi laughed. "The name came about because many of these graves belong to people who died suddenly with their boots on, like in a gunfight," Mimi explained. "This was truly a 'Wild, Wild, West' town!"

Mimi tied the shoelaces on her red tennis shoes. "Now I'm ready," she said. "Let's look at the tombstones. I hear they are great reading!"

"Born and died...born and died...born and died...that doesn't sound too interesting to me," Christina complained. "Isn't that what is usually written on tombstones?"

"Not here," answered Mimi. "Let's take a look."

Between the scrubby bushes and prickly cacti, they found the grave of one Lester Moore. A rugged tombstone stood among a pile of rocks.

Mimi said, "Look at that inscription!"

Christina started to giggle, then stopped. "Does that mean poor Les died from four shots by a 44-caliber pistol?"

"That's exactly right," Papa replied.

"You know what I wonder," Grant said, chucking a rock across the graveyard at a shady palo verde tree, "Why is everybody's middle name RIP?"

Papa laughed. "That means 'Rest in Peace', and it's on a lot of tombstones, not just ones in Boot Hill," he explained. "That's a really good question, actually!"

Something else immediately grabbed Grant's attention. "Papa!" he called out, pointing to a large gravesite piled high with rocks. "Here's where the gunfighters at the OK Corral are buried—those McLaury guys and Billy Clanton!" Mimi, Papa, and Christina hurried over to see three rickety tombstones standing at attention over a lumpy pile of jagged boulders.

Mimi said, "This is a desolate place to end up, even for a gunslinger." She wiped the sweat from her forehead with a bright yellow bandana as she surveyed the grave and the barren hills beyond. "Heat, dust, dirt, and endless desert," she added.

Christina circled around to see some of the other interesting tombstones. Suddenly, she stopped.

Gunfighter

THREE FINGER McGEE

Dead from lead at 33

Grant, walking beside her, said, "Christina, you look like you've seen a ghost!"

"Look at this tombstone!" Christina exclaimed. She couldn't believe her eyes. "Read the graffiti on the bottom. Do you see what I see? Grant read,

Gunfighter

**THREE
FINGER
McGEE**

**Dead from
lead at 33**

Beware, children!
I will rise from this
grave to scare you
like the dickens!

"Christina, did Three Finger's ghost write this?" Grant asked, his mouth open wide, his knees shaking.

"Is that message for us? Even in this heat, it gives me cold bumps!"

"You mean goose bumps. And there AREN'T any ghosts!" Christina insisted, even though chills ran down her spine. She tried to reassure Grant by saying, "Somebody wrote this, and I am going to find out who did it!" *And what does it mean?*

6 True Compadres

The next day, Christina and Grant visited the Tombstone Courthouse Museum. Papa and Mimi enjoyed cool glasses of lemonade at the diner across the street.

The kids wanted to see artifacts of the Old West like mining gear, wagons, and old photographs of cowboys and Indians. Grant headed directly to an exhibit of miners looking for silver and copper in the desert hills around Tombstone. "Treasure hunters!" he cried. "That's what I'm talking about!"

"You go ahead, I'll catch up," Christina said to Grant. "There's a special exhibit of Navajo paintings and pottery I want to see."

As she gazed at a chart showing important Navajo symbols, something caught Christina's eye. "Oh my gosh!" Christina cried. "Grant has GOT to see this!" She raced to the next room where Grant was playing with an interactive map showing the location of mines around Tombstone.

"Grant, you've got to come and see what I found!" Christina whispered. "Someone's trying to scare us!"

"The tombstone at the graveyard did that already," Grant said. "I don't want to look at more tombstones."

"No, this is something else!" Christina insisted. "Remember the animal drawing on the back of the SUV?"

"Yes," Grant answered. "Why?"

"Well, that strange animal is a coyote. The coyote is a trickster in the Navajo religion," Christina whispered even louder. "It's a symbol for something bad about to happen!"

Christina led Grant back to the Navajo exhibit.

"You're right, Christina," Grant agreed, examining the symbol on the chart. "It looks just like the animal drawn on our SUV!"

"Maybe we should tell Papa and Mimi," Christina said.

As they were leaving, they noticed two kids walking down the street. Christina recognized them as the two children from China Betty's restaurant. Christina waved to them and said, "Hi, remember us?"

"*Si*, you were at China Betty's," the girl with braids answered. "Your name is Christina."

"What's yours?" Christina asked.

"My name's Rosita Alonzo, and this is my brother, Jorge (hor-hay)," Rosita said, pointing to her bushy-haired, younger brother.

"Nice to meet you!" Christina replied. "This is my younger brother, Grant."

"Nice to meet you," Jorge and Rosita said in one voice.

"Where are you going?" Christina wanted to know.

"To the library," Rosita said. "We are returning library books."

"Can we walk with you?" Christina asked.

"Sure, it's not far," Rosita replied.

"I remember you said you were worried about your calf," Christina remarked, wanting to find out more about the strange happenings around this town.

"*Si.* So far she isn't sick," Rosita answered. "I thought she was for a day or two—when other cattle were getting sick."

"How long has this been going on—the cattle getting sick?" Christina asked.

"About a month or two," Jorge said. "That's when my dad started talking about it."

"I am really worried," Rosita said, pulling on one of her braids, "because my father is worried. He can't hide his feelings. When he sits down to supper, he always looks anxious. And—"

"And what?" Christina pressed her new friend for more information.

"Maybe you better NOT tell her," Jorge blurted out.

"Not tell us what?" Grant said, urging Jorge to say what he was thinking.

"Are you in danger?" Christina asked. "Please tell us. Maybe we can help!"

"Christina's really good at solving mysteries," Grant said. "If there is a mysterious problem, she can solve it."

Rosita and her brother looked at each other, as if seeming to have a silent understanding. Then Rosita said in a low voice, "Well, you have to promise not to laugh!"

"We won't laugh, I promise," Christina said.

Rosita said, "A true *compadre*, a true friend, would not laugh."

"All right, all right," Christina nodded, impatient to get to the heart of the matter.

Rosita looked around her to make sure there wasn't anyone besides the kids nearby. Then she said matter-of-factly, "We heard ghosts."

"No!" Christina said, as she bit her lip to hide a smile. "There are no such things!"

"We did hear ghosts," Jorge said firmly. "In a creepy old ghost town not far from my father's ranch."

"I believe you!" Grant cried. "I believe in ghosts! One even wrote us a message yesterday!"

"What?" Rosita asked. "You are not being haunted too?"

"That was NO ghost," Christina insisted, "just someone who wrote a dumb message on one of the tombstones in Boot Hill. It told us to beware because the ghost would rise from the grave and scare us one day. What was it like with your ghosts?"

Rosita replied, "It was evening, and dark shadows were everywhere. Jorge and I were on our way back from town. We stopped to rest by the old well in Eureka Gulch—"

"That's the name of the ghost town near our ranch," Jorge interrupted.

"A weird wind was blowing," Rosita continued. "It sounded just like owls. It went,

'WHOOOOO! WHOOOO!'

That's when we heard scary voices coming from inside an old wreck of a building. One mean-sounding voice said, 'All the water in Sunshine Gap will be bad. No one will want to live there!' Then another low voice said, 'All the horses and cattle ARE getting sick! No one will be able to stop it!'"

Jorge added, "All I could think about was my colt and my father's cattle!"

"And I thought of Spotty, my calf!" Rosita said. "We got so scared we ran all the way home!"

"Did you tell your parents?" Christina asked.

"Yes, but I think it just made them more worried," Rosita answered. "My father tried to comfort us by saying that the ghosts were just two men talking about cattle getting sick."

Rosita shrugged her shoulders. "But," she continued, "I didn't feel any better because it was the tone of their voices that gave me the shivers—just like two nasty ghosts!"

7 The Pits of Mining

Back at their motel, Christina and Grant told Mimi and Papa their findings about the coyote symbol at the museum, and Rosita and Jorge's ghost story.

"It sounds like you've got a mystery on your hands," Mimi said. "Where we visit next may help you to know more about the mysterious problems here in Sunshine Gap."

"Besides, a change of scenery might just be the best thing right now," Papa suggested. "How about a trip to Tombstone Canyon? Mimi's friend, Dr. Perez, has offered to give us a tour of the Bisbee, Arizona area. Bisbee is an old copper mining town built on the slopes of the Tombstone Canyon."

"Bizzz beee...bizzz beee," Grant said, making buzzing sounds and jabbing his hands all around Christina's head. "Sounds like a busy place for bees to me!"

"Grant!" Christina cried. "You're bugging me!" She grabbed Grant's bony wrists as they both began to giggle at her unintentional joke.

Mimi said, "Okay, kids, back to what Papa was saying. My friend, Dr. Maria Perez, is a mining engineer. She knows all about the mining that's been done around here. And she's a conservationist."

"What does that mean?" Grant asked.

"It means she knows a lot about mines," Papa said, "and how to protect the land, air, and water from the pollution mines can bring."

The family met Dr. Perez at a 1950s-style diner called Dot's Diner. Soon everyone was perched on stools at the counter, munching on thick hamburgers and crispy fries while a jukebox played early rock and roll music.

Dr. Perez said that Bisbee used to be one of the most important mining centers in the country. The town grew quickly because there was so much work to be done, and money to be made mining the copper.

When the mine dried up, the town's people moved away to find work elsewhere.

"Bisbee would have truly died," Dr. Perez remarked, "if the county courthouse weren't located here. Lately, the town has come alive again as artists, tourists, and craftspeople find treasures of a different sort in Bisbee."

She turned to the kids. "So, how would you like to tour a real mine?"

"You mean go down inside one?" Grant asked.

"Yes, we can ride a train down into the pit," Dr. Perez replied. "It's a great way to learn how mining was done here in the Old West."

"AWESOME!"

Grant cried. "How cool is that!"

"Let's go!" Christina exclaimed.

Dr. Perez led her guests to the Queen Mine and signed everyone up for the tour. At the changing house, everyone was outfitted in slickers, helmets, and miner's headlamps.

Grant's helmet was way too big for him. It wobbled whenever he turned his head.

"You look like a bobble-head," Christina said, as she jabbed her finger at his helmet, making it jiggle.

Grant jumped and butted his helmet against Christina's. "I'll bobble you back!" he cried.

"Stop it, you two!" Mimi ordered. "Act civil or you will be in major trouble!"

"Are we in 'miner' trouble now?" Grant asked with a grin as he tapped his helmet. "Get it, Mimi?"

Mimi smiled and straightened her own helmet. "I get that you're a silly boy!" she said.

Outfitted for their journey, the group then boarded the mining train, which rumbled 1,500 feet down into the pit of the mine. Christina and Grant clung to the sides of their seat, as the train lurched forward into the black hole ahead of them, lit only by dim, sickly yellow light bulbs.

CLINK! CLANK!

Suddenly, the train shuddered and slid over the edge into a deep tunnel that seemed to have no end. The air got cooler and cooler, and the pit got blacker and blacker. At the bottom of the mine, the tour leader guided the group through the cavernous, black tunnel. As everyone examined their surroundings, miner's lamps shot rays of light in every direction.

In the dark, the kids trailed their group, peering into inky holes in the shadowy walls. For the moment, their headlamps provided the only light.

Suddenly, Christina's elbow accidentally whacked Grant's helmet. It flew off his head and clattered onto the floor. Darkness swallowed everything.

"Christina!" Grant screamed. "I can't see anything! Where are you?"

Christina turned around sharply, her lamplight beaming on Grant and his fallen helmet. She grabbed the helmet and pushed it down on his head.

"Thanks a lot!" Grant breathed with a sigh of relief. "That's the darkest darkness I've ever seen!"

The kids hurried to join the rest of the tour group. Grant whispered, his voice shaking, "With no light, I felt for an instant like I was in a tomb!" He turned his head so that his miner's lamp found Christina's face. "What if we saw the ghost of somebody who died down here?"

"Let's not talk about ghosts now," Christina complained, her eyes blinded by Grant's light beam. "I've had enough for a while. Wait until we get back to Sunshine Gap!"

Dr. Perez joined the two kids as they walked back to the train for the ascent out of the mine. "Did I hear you say 'ghosts'? Have you seen one down here?"

Christina said, "No, ma'am. But we've heard of some strange happenings in Sunshine Gap." Christina then told Dr. Perez about Sunshine Gap's problems of questionable water, sick cattle, and the ghostly remarks heard by their friends in a ghost town.

"Well, some of those problems are very real," Dr. Perez said, as she settled in her seat on the train, "and not the work of ghosts. There are several reasons why the water could be bad and why the cattle are getting sick. One reason could be the fact that Sunshine Gap used to have copper mines in its vicinity."

"Oh?" Christina replied, sliding into the seat next to Dr. Perez.

"In the old days," Dr. Perez began, "mining was not done with the environment in mind. Chemicals, toxic materials, and waste products were left behind when the mines were abandoned. Water seeping from an old mine is often polluted when it enters streams and wells. People and cattle drink it and get sick...or worse."

"Boy!" Grant said, "That's really 'the pits' of mining! Scarier than this pit!"

"Yes," Dr. Perez replied. "And much more scary than ghosts."

Christina agreed. Toxic water was scarier than ghosts. *Was it pollution from the old mines near Sunshine Gap that was causing the cattle to get sick?*

8 Artifact or Artifice?

That evening, Papa, Mimi, Christina, and Grant returned to their motel at Sunshine Gap. The next morning, Papa rented horses from a local stable and led the kids and their friends, Rosita and Jorge, on a riding trip to a nearby ghost town, Hendersonville, just outside of Tombstone. Mimi, who was not excited about riding a horse all day, decided to stroll about Tombstone.

Hendersonville thrived in the mining heydays of the 1890s, but was now completely abandoned. Unlike Bisbee, its residents didn't find a way to restore new life to the town after its mine dried up.

As the kids rode the slowly plodding horses along the desert path to Hendersonville, they searched for cattle brands on the sides of the animals they passed. Growing up on a ranch, Jorge and Rosita knew about brands. They explained branding, or "calling" animal brands. Jorge told Grant that ranchers put the brands on their cows and horses to identify them. Each rancher has his own brand.

"See, our horses have the same brand," Rosita said, pointing at the design on the left flank of her mount. "An M lying sideways—that's read as Lazy M. Just like the restaurant where we ate was called Lazy H. Do you remember the sign had an H leaning sideways?"

"There are some steers over there," Papa said, pointing to cattle behind a fence. "Can you read their brand?"

Grant said, "It looks like a 'B' that's connected to a 'J' twice the size of the 'B'."

"Good description," Papa said. "Who do you think has a brand like that in town?"

"Big Jim!" Christina guessed.

"You're right," Jorge said.

They rounded a small hill and came upon the remains of Hendersonville. Very little was left of it except a few old stone buildings with caved-in roofs and a mineshaft leading into the side of the hill.

"Can we go in the buildings?" Grant asked.

"I don't see any 'No Trespassing' signs," Papa answered. "So we can. That's one of the rules of the ghost town code of ethics."

"Huh?" Grant asked. "What's that?

Papa said, "It's a set of sensible rules that visitors to ghost towns should respect. For example, other rules include not damaging or removing anything at a ghost town so other visitors can appreciate what's left. Of course, obvious trash like candy wrappers can be removed."

"OK, Papa," Grant answered, "We won't collect any souvenirs."

With warnings from Papa to watch out for crumbling roofs, the kids dismounted and explored the old buildings. Shrubs snaked up through broken floorboards. A lizard poked its head out from behind a toppled ceiling beam on a tattered wooden porch. Grant bent over to get a closer look at it.

Grant yelled. He leaped up, holding his bottom. He turned around to face a rotund barrel cactus with a piece of his pants dangling from one of its sharp needles.

"Are you OK?" Christina asked, turning Grant around to check the damage. She noticed just a little scratch on his skin but began to giggle when she saw the gaping hole in his pants!

"Papa will 'patch you up' right away," Christina said, smiling.

"I guess I do need a 'cactus patch'," Grant said, "and not the kind that grows in the desert!"

The kids continued exploring the rickety old buildings. *CREAK!* The door to an old bank offered a squeaky welcome. They lifted their feet gingerly over the debris scattered around the doorway.

All four kids grabbed each other and whirled around.

"Ghosts?" Grant asked as he watched the door eerily creak back open. "I thought I heard some footsteps!"

"It's just the wind!" Christina exclaimed. "Don't let your imagination run wild!" She couldn't admit that the slamming door had scared her too! They tiptoed further into the old building. Behind the cashier's window, a yellowed calendar showing the months of

What was that noise?

1929 still hung on the wall. However, on an old bench, Christina found something that indicated it wasn't ghosts that inhabited this place.

Christina pointed to two greasy paper plates and two brown-stained white coffee cups. She said, "These certainly aren't artifacts from the old days. This trash is disgusting!" As Christina lifted the plate to dispose of it, Rosita saw something brown slither from under the plate on to Christina's sleeve.

"Christina!" Rosita shouted. "Hold still! A scorpion!"

Christina froze in horror as the insect crawled from her sleeve to the back of her hand. It lifted its tail, just about to strike.

WHOOSH!

Jorge whipped off his hat and swiped it across Christina's hand, sending the scorpion flying across the room.

"EEWWWW!" Christina cried. She shook from head to toe. "Thank you, Jorge," she said, leaning against an old chair to regain her composure. "Those things are scary!"

Grant looked at the cup Christina picked up and said, "Now THIS scares me! Look! Three fingers and another warning!"

Christina turned over the cup and saw the drawing was done quickly with a ball point pen. This was clearly not the work of any real ghost of the dead gunslinger Three Fingers McGee. *Was the cup with the drawing just a sick joke or a real threat—artifact and NOT artifice?*

9 Bad Medicine or Bad Dream?

The next day, Mimi took Christina and Grant with her to shop at a local Indian jewelry and crafts store. Grant wanted to buy a silver belt buckle, while Christina wanted an Indian bracelet.

The store was in an old adobe building with a shady wooden front porch. Colorful Navajo rugs and blankets woven in stunning patterns hung from the walls. Straw baskets and earth-colored pottery were stacked on the shelves.

An old Indian with a beaded headband sat cross-legged on a rug. He hummed a strange sad tune as he carved a small piece of wood. Christina stopped to admire his carving. She gasped. The shape of the carving looked strangely familiar!

"How do you do?" Christina said, bending down to be near the Indian. "My name's Christina. What's your name?"

The Indian's face broke into a pensive smile as he said, "My name is Sam Begay."

"What are you carving, Mr. Begay?" Christina asked, thinking how the carving looked just like the drawing on the back of the SUV.

"A coyote," the Indian replied as he continued to carve.

"What's it for?" Grant piped up from behind Christina.

"The coyote is a magical animal," the Indian said, still carving away. "Coyote says change is coming—and it might not be good."

"Why are you carving it?" Christina asked.

"Because I had a dream," the Indian replied.

"Did something bad happen in your dream?" Christina whispered, as she bent even closer to hear the Indian's low voice.

"Yes," the Indian replied. "In my dream, it was night, with a full moon. A coyote was howling on a hilltop. Then, two ghosts poured brown, bad medicine into a clear, pure stream. The cattle drank from the stream and began to cry big, black tears."

Christina said to Grant, "I wonder if the cattle are crying because they are sick?"

Just then, Big Jim Wilcox walked by, smoking a cigar.

"Well, if it isn't Christina and Grant from the restaurant," he said. "Are you still worried about our sick cattle?"

"Mr. Begay was just telling us a dream, Mr. Wilcox," Grant said.

"Old Indian Begay is always telling stories, kids," Big Jim said, throwing his cigar into the street. "Don't pay too much attention to him."

"Oh, Mr. Wilcox," Christina said. "We saw your brand on some cattle—the B connected to the big J— when we went riding to Hendersonville."

"I guess you would," Big Jim said as he strode into the store. "My ranch is near there."

Just then, Mimi walked out, carrying a shopping bag full of gifts for the family back home. Big Jim tipped his cowboy hat to her and said, "Howdy, ma'am. I see you like our jewelry. Did you try the free sample coffee? I'm getting a cup of java now."

"Oh, I did, thanks," Mimi answered. "It's delicious!" She turned back to the kids. "Are you ready to go now?"

"We haven't bought anything," Christina replied. "We can come back later. I was much more interested in what the Indian, Mr. Begay, had to say."

"You'll have to tell me later," Mimi said.

The kids returned with Mimi to their motel where Mimi took her purchases out of her shopping bag to show Papa.

"What's this?" Mimi asked, as she fished a small wooden piece from her bag. "I didn't buy this carving. I'd better return it."

Christina and Grant froze when they saw the carving. It was Mr. Begay's coyote!

"I think that was meant for us, Mimi," Christina said, gulping. She turned to Grant. "I think it's another coyote warning like the drawing on the SUV," she whispered to Grant. "I think Mr. Begay put it in the bag!"

Christina's mind was full of questions. Why did Big Jim Wilcox dismiss the old Indian's words? Could he be the "ghost" of Three Finger McGee? His ranch was near the old ghost town of Hendersonville. It would be easy for him to put a coffee cup there. Did the Indian draw the figure on the SUV? He had to be the one to give us the carved coyote to warn us—for good reasons or bad? Were the coyotes threats or hints to be careful?

Much more serious questions also popped into Christina's head. *Did the Indian's dream mean that the water was being polluted by the "ghosts of the past," the miners of long ago with their harmful mining practices? Or, worse yet, was it being deliberately poisoned by sinister people now?*

10 Strange Happenings at Eureka Gulch

Papa decided to take Christina and Grant on a camping trip. Mimi did not go along, choosing instead to go see the world's largest rose tree at the Rose Tree Inn. Christina, ever the sleuth, thought that a camping trip was the perfect opportunity to investigate whether or not there really were "ghosts" in Eureka Gulch polluting the water and sickening the cattle.

"Papa," Christina begged, "can we go camping in Eureka Gulch?"

"Why Eureka Gulch?" Papa asked. "There are plenty of places to go camping."

"NOT THAT PLACE where Rosita and Jorge heard strange ghost-like voices?" Grant wailed. "I KNOW

YOU, CHRISTINA, YOU ARE JUST TRYING TO PROVE THERE ARE NO GHOSTS!"

"Well, yes," Christina admitted with a sly grin. "We might as well have some adventure as well as some fun!"

"Papa!" Grant cried. "She's trying to scare me."

"No, I'm not," Christina said. "Maybe you'll learn that there ARE no ghosts! Then you will have nothing to be afraid of."

Papa said, with a twinkle in his eye, "I think the campout will be good for the both of you. You both may be proven right!"

A long, bumpy horseback ride brought the trio into the desolate valley called Eureka Gulch. A copper mine once thrived there, creating a small town of prospectors. After the mining was over, the citizens moved away, leaving empty skeletons of their homes and work places. The bleached wooden houses, bank, saloon, and general store hung precariously on both sides of the valley walls. Beneath an old, weather beaten sign stating this was Eureka Gulch, population

3000, the skeleton of a steer could be seen, half buried in the sandy soil.

"Even though it's hot," Grant moaned, wiping the sweat from his forehead, "just looking at this place gives me the shivers."

"It might be better to camp on the outskirts of town," Papa said, "that way we can have a place with a good view of both the land and the town." It wasn't long before Papa selected a high spot on a hill overlooking the valley.

Grant, Christina, and Papa unpacked their gear and made a campfire. Around the crackling fire, they cooked some hotdogs and baked beans. As they feasted on a dessert of roasted marshmallows, they watched the setting sun cast a pinkish, golden glow on the town and distant mountains.

"Hey, Papa," Grant called. "What's the best thing to take into the desert?"

"Well, I don't know, Grant," Papa replied.   He sensed a joke was on the way.

"A thirst aid kit!" Grant shouted, falling over with giggles. Papa laughed and tickled Grant until he cried, "Uncle!"

Christina's mind was not on jokes. "Eureka Gulch is really beautiful at this time of day. It's not scary at all," Christina said, leaning against her saddle now lying next to her sleeping bag. "Let's go exploring in the town before it get's too dark."

"Okay," said Papa. "But make sure you have your cell phone and flashlight, Christina. I'll stay here with the horses. I'll watch where you go by following the beam from the flashlight. Be sure to call me if anything happens."

"I will, Papa," Christina promised.

"I'll make her!" Grant added.

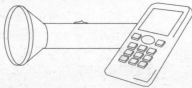

The kids wandered down what was once the main street of Eureka Gulch. They gazed up at the crumbling buildings around them. Going from house to house, they explored the ramshackle insides of what once were a person's home, a blacksmith's shop, and a general

It's dark out there!

store, careful not to trip over the debris around them. They found or heard nothing unusual. Before they knew it, the sun slipped under the horizon, leaving them in the dusty twilight.

"Now it's getting spooky," Grant said. "Maybe we better go back to our camp."

"It's cool, though," Christina noted, as they walked down Main Street. "Look how dark it is. There are no streetlights, only the light of the nearly full moon."

"And the stars! I've never seen so many stars!" Grant cried.

"That's because there're no city lights around," Christina said, as she spotted the old well that Rosita had mentioned. She hoped she could recreate Rosita's situation by sitting near the well. She sat down, but try as she might, the only things Christina heard were the moan of the wind, the rustle of a few tumbleweeds rolling down the street, and the lonely howl of a coyote in the distance. The only new things she saw were a rabbit leaping among moonbeams, and a big, lazy tarantula meandering across the street.

"I have to admit," Christina said, "this gives me the CREEPS, especially that spider! But we haven't seen any ghosts, even though it's not hard to imagine they're around! We might as well go back." Christina pointed to a distant slope, adding, "I can see Papa's campfire over there in the distance."

"Christina! That's NOT Papa's fire," Grant whispered. He pointed 90 degrees in the opposite direction. "His fire is up there!"

"What?" Christina said, looking around to get her bearings. "I think you are right, Grant! We passed that old bank on the way here.

"Keep the flashlight low," Christina commanded, as she leaped up. "We're going to investigate that new campfire."

"We better call Papa," Grant warned.

"The campfire may be nothing to worry about," Christina said, changing direction. "Let's check it out first."

With Grant reluctantly in tow, Christina trotted in the direction of the strange campfire, careful to stay in the shadows. She whispered to Grant, "I remember Papa saying that Eureka Gulch's old mine was up here somewhere. Maybe the campfire is next to the mineshaft." Leaving the ghost town, they scrambled up the hill. They could smell coffee warming over the distant fire.

"So far, so good," Christina whispered to Grant, "ghosts don't drink coffee!"

"Good!" Grant whispered. "We still better stay behind the rocks, Christina. I remember in the movies the cowboys always kept their heads down and hid behind rocks."

"No one's going to shoot at us," Christina whispered back. "But we do need to keep hidden. We don't want anyone to know we're here."

The kids crept among the shadows and rocks. By the flickering light of the campfire, they could barely see two ghostly figures walk out of the old mineshaft. "Let's stop and listen," Christina said. "We should hear their voices from here."

11 Ghoulish Prowlers

The two kids spied on the ghostly characters at the mineshaft. "Even though we can't see their faces," Christina whispered, "maybe we can learn what they're doing here at this hour!"

The figures moved quietly back and forth, carrying sacks and equipment into the mine with a shiny red wheelbarrow. One shadowy figure passed a hurricane lamp to the other man, causing the light to flicker briefly on both of them. Christina whispered to Grant, "They do look like ghosts in this light. But they're human. See, one is drinking a cup of coffee."

"Shhh!" Grant whispered, not wanting to admit Christina was right. "They're starting to talk!"

"You reckon we have enough of this stuff?" the smaller man asked the taller one.

"More than enough!" the taller man answered. "It should take care of things. I guess we're ready for Tuesday night. We'll come back to finish the job then."

At that moment, the wind picked up, making a low, moaning sound. The kids couldn't overhear the conversation. "That wind sounds scary," Grant whispered to Christina.

Scarier still, Grant had forgotten to keep the flashlight low, exposing the brightness of the light to the men at the mine—and Christina and Grant did not know it! They looked away from the men to whisper to each other. Christina asked Grant, "What did that man mean about taking care of things? What was in the bags they carried into the mine?"

Before Grant could answer, a voice screamed from behind them,

"YAHHHH!

I am Three Finger McGee!" A shadowy figure then leaped out from behind a cactus, with one arm raised. It charged at the kids.

"HELLLLLLLP!"

Grant yelled, as he jumped up. "CHRISTINA! RUN! Three Finger McGee's after us!"

The two kids ran like wildfire back to the town. "Faster, Grant!" Christina panted, as she thrust the flashlight in front of her to see the trail ahead. "He's still following us!"

Grant stumbled on a rock and plummeted to the ground. "Christina! Help!"

Christina, hardly breaking her stride, bent down and grabbed Grant's hand. She yanked him up and the two kids raced down the path to town. Christina yelled, "Papa! Papa!" as loud as she could as she huffed and puffed, sprinting with Grant in tow. *She didn't think her grandfather could hear her from this distance, but she thought it might stop the "ghost" from following them!*

12 Finds in the Mine

It seemed like it took forever for the kids to get back to the ghost town. For a moment, the old town even looked like a haven as the kids frantically searched for a hiding place inside the old store. They burrowed down among the debris behind the store's counter.

"I don't hear anything!" Christina whispered. "I think he's gone!"

Christina moved to a broken window and peeped out into the moonlit street. In the distance, she saw a truck drive downhill from the mine and lumber out of town.

RIIING! RIIING!

Christina's cell phone shrieked. Both kids jumped.

"Answer it!" Grant whispered as Christina feverishly searched her pockets. "Somebody might hear!"

She finally found the phone in her back pocket. "Hello?" Christina whispered into the receiver.

"Christina? Where are you? I can't see your flashlight!" Papa asked.

"Papa!" Christina cried out. "We're in the ghost town. There were two men at the mine. They must have seen our flashlight. One man calling himself Three Finger McGee jumped out from behind a cactus and chased us away!"

"Is he still after you?" Papa asked, his voice suddenly sounding worried.

"No, we outran him," Christina said. "I think I just saw their truck leave town."

"Good!" Papa said. "Look carefully around you and keep your flashlight from shining in the direction of the mine. And keep it low. I'm heading down the path to meet you. Get back here ASAP!"

Christina and Grant peered into the moonlit street in both directions and raced back to their camp.

Papa greeted them with big bear hugs. The kids told him about seeing the two men drinking coffee and carrying things but didn't mention what they had heard them say.

"So, you don't know what the two men were doing?" Papa asked.

"No," Christina answered. "We couldn't hear all they said because of the blowing wind."

"It's strange that they were there, but at least you know they are two real-life men and not ghosts!" Papa commented. "That is a step in the right direction."

Christina said, "The man calling himself Three Finger McGee must be the one who left the warnings on the tombstone and on the cup. He really did try to scare us like he said he would!"

"Well, he sure scared me!" Grant cried. "He looked like a real ghost."

"You didn't recognize him?" Papa asked.

"No, it was too dark and happened too fast," Christina replied. "He did seem to be on the big side. Maybe he was the taller of the two men at the mineshaft." The kids climbed into their sleeping bags although they were still excited from the night's events.

"Can we go back to that mine in the morning, Papa?" Christina asked. "If no one is there, we might be able to see what they were storing in the mine. That might tell us what they're doing."

"OK," Papa said. "But only if no one is there, and there are no 'No Trespassing' signs. Those guys just might be storing stuff and don't want a bunch of kids around getting into trouble."

The next morning, Papa drove Christina and Grant to the old mine. In the light of day, nothing appeared scary and no one was around. There were no signs forbidding anyone to be on the land. The mine just seemed like a deep hole in the slope of the hill. The kids and Papa spotted the ashes of the campfire from the night before.

"Someone's been here recently," Papa said. He sifted the ashes with his boot and kicked a newly used foam cup, brown stained and still smelling of coffee.

"Can we go in the mine, Papa?" Grant asked.

"Let me go with you," Papa answered, as he flipped on the flashlight.

The trio crept into the mine. Inside, the mine actually had two shafts going in different directions. Grant and Papa started down one shaft. Christina, following, decided to take the other instead. She walked about five yards, when the beam of her flashlight fell on some lumpy bags. A skull and crossbones was printed on the side of each bag. The word POISON was written in bold below the crossbones.

"PAAAAAAAPA!" Grant suddenly screeched from the other mineshaft.

Christina could hear Grant screaming and racing out of the other mineshaft. She turned and charged back to the opening, only to be hit by hundreds of black flying objects brushing her hair, her arms, and her back!

"PAAAPA!" Christina shrieked as she shook a struggling animal out of her hair. She waved her arms and danced in a circle, frantically trying to get away from the creatures.

"Bats!" Papa yelled as he made huge swooping motions to scare the bats from the kids. "I hate bats!"

"Bats!" Grant screamed, his arms flailing at the frightened animals. "I want to bat them with my baseball bat!"

In the shock of fighting off bats, Christina forgot about seeing the bags marked POISON until later when they rode back home. She didn't want to say anything to Papa yet. She was reminded of the old Indian's dream. Mr. Begay had seen two ghosts pour 'bad medicine' into the streams. *Were those bags she saw marked POISON the bad medicine? And were the two men the ghosts in Mr. Begay's dream?*

13 Hatching a Plan

The kids and Papa returned to Sunshine Gap and their motel. While Papa took a nap, the kids met Jorge and Rosita at the pizza shop. They found a table for four and dug into the thick pizzas dripping with cheese. Christina told Rosita and Jorge about the old Indian's dream, the two men at the mine, and being chased. Christina then mentioned the bags of poison she found just as Grant was terrified by the bats.

"You didn't tell Papa?" Grant asked.

"No," Christina said. "It's our secret. Besides, that poison might be used for some good purpose. It might have nothing to do with the water. We don't know." After taking a gulp of tangy lemonade, Christina said, "BUT, it could be like the old Indian dreamed. Maybe they're pouring 'bad medicine' into the water."

"How do we know they're the same two 'ghosts' we heard when we were at the well?" Rosita asked.

"Those two we heard were definitely bad guys up to no good! What did the voices of the two guys you saw sound like?"

Grant said, "Just like two men talking normally. Nothing REALLY scary. Except when Three Finger McGee jumped out and chased us! Maybe it was Three Finger McGee's ghost coming back to scare us. The notes on the tombstone and the coffee cup promised he would."

"We won't know for sure if those guys we saw at the mine are up to something bad unless you and Jorge recognize their voices," Christina remarked.

"We didn't get to see them that clearly," Grant reminded Christina. "We couldn't see their faces."

Christina said, "One way we can solve this mystery is for all four of us to go back to the mine and see if we can find out something more."

"AGAIN, Christina? How can we do that?" Grant asked his sister, as he scrunched his eyebrows into knots. "I don't think Papa would want to go back there for another camping trip."

"I know what we can do," Rosita said, clasping her hands together. "The Eureka Gulch mine is near my father's property—just near the boundary line. Why don't we invite you two for some camping on our ranch on Tuesday night, the night the men said they'd be back..."

". . . And all four of us can make camp near the boundary, and then sneak over at night to the mine?" Christina continued, a big grin on her face.

"Yeah, maybe we can catch those two guys in the act!" Grant said.

With their next big adventure planned, they began to talk about other things. Christina asked Rosita and Jorge about the brands used by the local ranchers.

"What's yours?" Christina asked.

"The Circle A, an 'A' inside a circle," Rosita answered.

"And some others around here?" Christina wanted to know.

"A weird dude called Dead Eye," Rosita said, "has an eye shape with a 'D' inside, where the colored part of the eye is."

"I remember that guy from the restaurant," Grant said, grabbing another piece of pizza. "His eyelids didn't close much when he spoke. He sort of stared."

Rosita said, "It makes him seem like an ice man." Rosita then returned to the topic of local ranchers' brands. "You remember Big Jim's, right?"

"Yeah, that's an easy one to read," Christina replied. Then she added as an afterthought, "Big Jim doesn't think much of Mr. Begay, does he?"

"You're right," Jorge said. "Big Jim might be afraid of Indian Begay."

"Why?" Christina asked.

"The old Indian is a shaman who seems to know everything going on in the physical world AND the spiritual world," Rosita said. "That sometimes scares guys like Big Jim who don't know anything about dreams and psychic stuff. Who knows, maybe Big Jim has something to hide?"

14 Something Fishy is Going On!

"With the old Indian's story and the mystery at Eureka Gulch, a lot has happened to us since we last met. What's been happening to you?" Christina asked Rosita, as she finished off her second piece of pizza.

"We've had a lot happen too," Rosita murmured. "But I can't say that it was fun or even good."

"It must not be good," Christina sympathized. "You've hardly touched your pizza!"

"My colt got sick," Jorge cried, as tears welled up in his eyes. He put his elbows on the table and covered his eyes. He didn't want to start bawling like a baby in front of his friends.

"No! That's awful," Grant said, patting his friend on the back. "How is your horse now?"

"He's better," Jorge said, sniffing and wiping his nose. "Now I really watch the water he drinks."

"The results came back from testing the well water," Rosita informed Christina and Grant. "The water was toxic like we thought. The tester who took the sample said more study is needed. He still doesn't know what caused the water to go bad."

"Why not, Rosita?" Christina asked.

"I guess it's not the usual runoff from mines in this area," Rosita answered. "Something else may have been added to the water, or the usual diluted runoff toxins could have been made more poisonous."

"It looks like something fishy is going on then, not something natural," Christina concluded. "The old Indian's dream may be right on!"

"*Si*," Rosita said. "The work of someone bad with bad medicine. Who would want to hurt us and the other people in this town?"

"Did your father tell the sheriff, Big Jim?" Christina asked.

"He did," Jorge replied. "But he hasn't done anything that we know of."

"Christina," Jorge cried, "what's going to happen if all our water gets poisoned? I don't want to move away!"

Rosita added, "My father and mother are already talking about moving somewhere else if we can't make a go of the new well being dug."

Both Alonzo kids looked depressed. **Flaccid** expressions of hopelessness dulled their faces while they hunched over their food. Neither kid had eaten much pizza.

I've lost my appetite!

Just then, a roar from a motorcycle made everyone look outside the pizza parlor. The rider was a tall man with a tattoo on his left arm. He shut down his bike, removed his helmet, and swaggered into the pizza parlor. The rider looked over at Christina and Grant. His eyes narrowed. He then saw Rosita and Jorge, and said in a rough, loud voice, "Sorry to hear about your colt! Seems like a lot of animals are taking sick. Best bet is for folks to skedaddle."

"Uh, thanks," Jorge said as the man moved on to the counter to order some pizza. "Easy for you to say."

"That's a local bad guy named Dusty," Rosita whispered to Christina and Grant. "I wonder if he would poison the water. If there's trouble in town, he usually has a part in it."

"I recognize him," Christina whispered back. "He was at the restaurant the day we arrived. Like Big Jim, he's big enough to be the guy that chased us."

"By telling us to skedaddle," Jorge added, "it looks like he would like to see everyone leave town."

"All of us leaving would make our home another ghost town," Rosita said, shaking her head.

"I wonder why he would want everyone to leave," Christina pondered as she swallowed the last of her lemonade. "None of you should leave."

Christina knew that other towns became ghost towns because something important to the town vanished. It didn't matter whether it was clean water, copper, gold, or silver. Christina wanted to do all she could to make sure this wouldn't happen to Sunshine Gap. She felt sure that the mystery at Eureka Gulch was tied to the pollution problem of Sunshine Gap. *Solving this mystery just might keep the water clean and save the town!*

15 A Dead Ringer for Dead Eye?

"Before we go, we should make a list of camping equipment we need," Grant said to the other kids as he tossed his dirty pizza plate and cup in the trash barrel by their table.

"Shhh!" Christina whispered, pointing at Dusty still in line to order food. "He could be one of our suspects! Let's talk about the new cowboy movie that's supposed to be playing at the theater."

The kids discussed the movie while spying on Dusty. From time to time, Dusty twisted around and looked at the kids with an odd grin. When his turn at the cash register came, he ordered three mini pizzas to go. He then held up three fingers.

"Christina," Grant whispered. "Did you see that?"

"What?" Christina answered.

"Dusty held up three fingers to show how many pizzas he wanted but he didn't hold up three fingers the usual way, like holding the thumb over the baby finger. He held up them up like this." Grant held up his thumb, forefinger and middle finger, bending back the ring and baby finger. "Just like the ghost of Three Finger McGee!"

"Shhh!" Christina hissed again.

"What time will that movie play tonight?" Rosita asked blandly, as the other kids **covertly** watched the gloved motorcycle rider saunter out of the restaurant with his takeout pizza. When he was gone, Rosita whispered, "Oh my gosh, Christina, I didn't think to tell you something when you talked about the ghost of Three Finger McGee. Dusty's only got three fingers on his right hand! He lost his ring finger and baby finger in a motorcycle accident. Most people don't know that because he always wears gloves."

Grant said, "I wonder if HE thinks he's the ghost of Three Finger McGee!"

"Well," Jorge replied, "He's one bad *hombre*! He sure acts like Three Finger McGee sometimes!"

After the kids made a list of things they needed to go camping, they said their goodbyes. Later that day, Mimi and Papa took Christina and Grant to buy the gear and equipment at a local store.

"Did you find everything?" Christina asked Grant, as she looked over her list.

"Yep," Grant answered. "I even found a battery for my digital camera."

"Good thinking," Christina said. "Maybe we can use the camera to collect some hard evidence. A good photo or video could be worth a million words!"

"I didn't think the store had batteries, but they do," Grant said. "They're over by the wheelbarrows."

"Wheelbarrows?" Christina asked Grant. "I wonder if that new wheelbarrow we saw at the mine was bought in this store!" As Christina paid for her purchases, she asked the clerk if anyone had bought a new wheelbarrow recently.

The clerk said, "Yes, someone did just last week."

"Who?" Christina asked, getting excited.

"I can't help you there," the clerk said. "I'm new here."

"Can you tell me what he looked like?" Christina wanted to know. "Any special features?"

"No—just average, not tall, or short," the clerk replied. "He was wearing sunglasses."

"Can you quickly draw a picture of his face? Please?" Christina asked, getting frustrated. "There are no other customers now."

"Well, OK," the clerk answered. "I used to study Art. I never forget a face." The clerk took a piece of paper out from behind the counter and sketched a very lifelike face.

"It looks like someone I've seen," Grant said, studying the picture.

"I wonder," Christina thought out loud, "without the sunglasses, could it be Dead Eye?"

"You're right, Christina!" Grant shouted, grabbing the paper to examine it more closely. "It could be a dead ringer for Dead Eye if the looks weren't so common."

"Dead Eye?" the clerk asked.

"Yeah," Grant answered. "The man's nickname. His eyelids stay open. He sort of stares. See, I'll show you." Grant stared straight ahead and opened his eyes as wide as he could. "Ow," he remarked, "that kinda hurts."

"Well, I didn't notice that," the clerk recalled. "I couldn't see his eyes because he wore those sunglasses that reflect back at you."

Christina and Grant thanked the clerk for his help, and left the store. Christina said, "Too bad we still don't know for sure if Dead Eye really did buy the wheelbarrow. Many guys could look like him — just an average guy. This picture is at best just a clue."

Grant said, "If we think he's our man, we can make this our MOST WANTED picture and hang it up in the motel room!"

Sweetening
16 the
Water

Back at the motel, Grant hung up the drawing looking like Dead Eye. "Hey, Christina," he said, "I wish I had the dartboard from Papa's house. I'd put Dead Eye on there and show him who's boss!" Grant danced about, pretending to launch darts at the picture.

"Yep," Christina replied, "we definitely have him in our sights!"

The next day, the kids got ready to go on their camping trip at the Alonzo ranch. Christina and Grant packed up their camping gear, food, and clothes. Papa helped them load the SUV, and it wasn't long before they drove through the Circle A Ranch gates.

They pulled up to the Alonzo house, a low lying brick house with a wide porch. Rosita, Jorge, and their father came out to greet Christina, Grant, Mimi, and Papa. After the greetings, Papa and Mimi hugged their grandkids. "Be careful out there," Mimi said, "and be sure to call if you need us!"

Grant whispered to Christina after Papa and Mimi drove away, "I think Papa's on to us. I think he knows we're doing more than just camping at the Alonzo ranch."

"I didn't tell him anything!" Christina said.

Mr. Alonzo brought two horses from the stable for Christina and Grant to ride. Jorge and Rosita rushed off to get their two horses.

"Is this your colt?" Grant asked, surprised when Jorge returned with a jet-black horse big enough to ride. It was already saddled.

"*Si*," Jorge said proudly. He patted the horse's shiny flank. "Isn't he great?" Jorge asked. "His name is Domino. He's still young, but I don't weigh much so I can ride him."

With a goodbye and thanks to Mr. Alonzo, the kids rode down a trail leading to the outskirts of the ranch. Reaching wide-open flatland, the kids raced their horses, and rode through a brook to cool off.

Rosita said to Jorge, "Look, the sun's setting. We should go to that spot near the Eureka Gulch mine to camp."

With a loud "HEYAAA!" to the horses, the four kids set off at a gallop across the barren fields to some distant hills. As the sound of her horse's hooves pounded beneath her, and the wind blew through her hair, Christina knew why Papa liked riding in the West so much. She loved it! For just a moment, she didn't care whether they found ghosts or solved the mystery!

Rosita and Jorge chose the side of a low hill on their ranch boundary as a campsite. "There are rocks here," Jorge said, pointing at the jagged boulders strewn about the hillside, "making a natural wall on three sides— almost an enclosed circle. We can build a campfire here, in the middle of the circle."

"No one will see the fire from the Eureka Gulch mineshaft even though it's just beyond this hill," Rosita added.

Grant dug a wide, shallow hole for a fire pit and dropped his shovel to admire his work. At that very moment, Domino pulled on his tether, backed up, lifted his tail, and pooped right into the pit!

Jorge burst out laughing. Grant fumed as Jorge pulled the horse away. "Domino!" Grant shouted. "Thank you very much! You're a party pooper and I AM POOPED. Now I have to dig another pit!"

"Don't forget to pooper scoop!" Christina said, laughing as she handed Grant his shovel.

Grant slapped his hand over his mouth. "Ugh! That really smells BAD!"

After Grant's cleanup, the kids built a fire and warmed up a pot of thick beef vegetable soup that Mrs. Alonzo had made for them. As the kids slurped their soup and munched on a hearty loaf of bread, they talked about their planned foray to the mineshaft.

After eating, the four kids scrambled up the rocky hillside. They each hid behind a boulder. Christina pointed the binoculars on the old mineshaft. She could barely make it out in the distance.

"It's about a half mile away," Jorge said, pointing as he spoke. "If we go by way of those rocks to the left, we will be able to stay hidden but still see what's happening."

"Where does your ranch boundary end?" Christina wanted to know. "It's best we stay on your side as much as possible!"

"See that large clump of shrubs, and the barbed wire fence running near it?" Jorge asked, again pointing to show the place. "That marks our boundary."

"So the mine really is just beyond the boundary!" Christina said. "Thank goodness—in case we have to hurry back!"

"It doesn't look like anyone's there now," Grant reported, squinting through his binoculars to get a clear view.

"We'll wait until dark and take another look," Rosita said, as she jumped over a rock to go back to the campsite.

"This'll be scary," Grant warned. "Christina, don't take any crazy chances or Papa will NEVER let us do anything like this again."

"Don't worry," Christina replied. "I'll be very careful!"

When it was totally dark, with only moonlight and starlight to brighten the way, the kids hiked back up the hill to their lookout post. They positioned themselves behind the boulders and sited the mine in their binoculars.

"There's a campfire!" Grant exclaimed.

"Let's get going," Christina suggested, "before they leave the mine."

The kids scrambled down the hill, and with Rosita in the lead, tiptoed into open territory, hiding behind each shrub, rock, and cactus they could find on their route to the mineshaft. Jorge then took the lead, whispering, "I know a gate in the barbed wire fence. It's over here."

Jorge struggled with the gate latch in the dark. He got it open, and the kids followed him through it to "enemy territory" where anything could happen.

Not too far from the mineshaft, the kids found four rocks large enough to hide behind while they spied on the two "ghosts." Grant took his digital camera from his jeans pocket and mounted it on the rock.

"Look!" Christina whispered to the other three kids as she peered through the binoculars. "The guys are coming out of the cave. One guy is carrying a sack marked POISON. The other has a lamp."

"I can't see who they are," Rosita said. "They have bandanas tied around their faces."

Grant whispered, "SHHH! I got the video going on the camera so we can catch voices and actions."

The kids watched in silence as the taller of the two men clearly said in a nasty voice, "It's time to sweeten the water!"

"That's the voice we heard at the well, Christina," Rosita gasped.

Christina was sure that "sweeten the water" could only mean that they were going to poison the water. Then and there, she decided to trust the dream of the old Indian.

17 Deeds in the Darkness!

Christina decided to retreat back to the gate leading to the Alonzo ranch. The kids could not be seen or heard this time! As she scrambled to leave, Grant pointed to his camera, and then made a thumbs up sign indicating he was still recording video, and that he had caught the taller man saying it was time to "sweeten the water."

Rosita, Jorge, and Grant watched the two men move to the right into the darkness. The light of their lamp revealed a mule tied to a bush. Grant hoped his camera would catch the men loading the sack on the mule's back.

Dashing through the dark, crouching among rocks and brush, Christina reached the gate. Suddenly, she heard a rustling sound. In the darkness, she could barely make out the two men leading the mule with the bag on its back. They were heading for the gate right next to her!

Christina scurried to the nearest boulder, crouching low behind it. Her heart was beating so loudly in her ears, she was sure the two men could hear it as they passed by. They came closer and closer. They carried the flickering hurricane lamp that dimly outlined their figures in the dark of the night.

As she waited, Christina wondered what Rosita, Grant, and Jorge were doing. Obviously they hadn't been caught or these guys wouldn't be arriving here so quickly. She hoped the kids overheard something that would help solve the mystery. Grant's videotaping could provide good evidence if they were going to poison the water!

The men drew closer. Christina strained to hear anything they might say.

"Do we need these bandanas tied around our faces?" the taller man asked the shorter one.

"We saw the kids spying on us last time," the shorter man said. "You never can be too careful."

"Don't worry. We gave them a good scare!" the taller man said.

Christina's heart pounded even louder and harder. She had heard that voice just recently! Was the taller guy the one who jumped out from behind the cactus and chased them?

"I think sweetening the water this time will really convince the people to move away," the short man said through the bandana tied about his face.

Just then, the rope securing the bag on the mule loosened and the bag nearly slipped off the animal's back. The taller man stepped over to tighten it. The shorter man held the lantern over the back of the mule to shine some light. It was enough light for Christina to make out the brand on the mule's flank.

Oh my gosh! Christina thought. That's Dead Eye's brand! He's got to be involved—even if he's not one of these guys! She watched as the taller man tightened the rope to secure the bag. The men then led the mule to the gate. *They were now trespassing on the Alonzo ranch. They had no right to be there. It was time to call for help!*

18 Trailing the Trespassers

Christina waited behind the boulder until the men were too far away to hear her voice. She was just about to call Papa when she heard more rustling in the dark! Her heart pounded. Who or what was this? A wild animal or another bad guy? Then she heard a familiar whisper. "Christina, where are you?" It was Grant!

"Here, over here by the gate," Christina answered, blowing out a huge sigh of relief. "Did you see the two guys come over here?"

"Yes," Rosita answered. "We decided to follow them as soon as we saw they were heading for our ranch! We knew we would catch up with you—if the two guys didn't find you first!"

"Thank goodness, they didn't!" Christina said. "I heard them just in time! One of the guys said they're the ones who scared us at the mine. And I recognized his voice. I just can't place it."

"Let's get going," Grant exclaimed. "We can't lose them! We need to see what they're doing with the poison."

"I'll call Papa," Christina said, "as soon as I know where those two guys are going!"

The kids followed the men, ducking behind bushes and talking in whispers so they weren't seen or heard.

"Where are they going?" Christina asked Rosita.

"Beyond that hill," Rosita answered, pointing to a distant rise. "It looks like they're heading to the creek that provides water for most of our cattle."

"Does the creek have a name?" Grant asked.

"Eureka Creek is what the ranchers call it," Jorge replied, "because it flows from the hills around Eureka Gulch."

"That would make it look like the poison is coming from the mine!" Christina concluded. "I had better call Papa — now!"

Christina quickly dialed Papa's number.

"Papa!" Christina whispered. "I'm OK. I'm with Rosita, Jorge, and Grant. We're on Alonzo land. But so are two guys with a mule! They're trespassing, and they are carrying a bag marked POISON! Rosita thinks they're taking the poison to the section of Eureka Creek that flows on their land. Maybe you should call the police!"

"Have you learned anything else?" Papa asked.

They're going that-a-way!

"Yes," Christina replied. "The mule has Dead Eye's brand on its flank. And I recognized the voice of one of the men when I heard him say they tried to scare us at the mine. I just can't remember where I heard it!"

"Are the men armed with guns?" Papa wanted to know.

"No," Christina said. "They're just carrying some shovels."

"Where are you now?" Papa asked.

Christina gave him the coordinates from the GPS device on her cell phone.

"I'm calling Mr. Alonzo right now," Papa said. "Put your phone on vibrate, so I can call you back."

Christina quickly adjusted her phone ringer. Within one minute, it began to buzz. It was Papa calling back.

"Christina," Papa said, "keep a safe distance away from the men and watch out for the other kids. We're calling the police. Mr. Alonzo, Mimi, and I will be out there right away."

"Come quietly!" Christina suggested. "And tell the police to ambush those guys!"

Christina closed her cell phone, and the kids continued to watch the two men and the mule. It looked more and more like they were heading to Eureka Creek, just as Rosita thought. *Surely the two men could be up to no good! Would the police and her grandparents arrive in time? Would the police catch the culprits in the act?*

19 Hitting Pay Dirt

As the kids continued to follow the men, they heard snatches of their conversation.

"When the Alonzos leave," the shorter man said, "we can finally get at the copper I found on this land. The Eureka Gulch mine wasn't dug far enough in this direction. There's a bonanza sitting under this dirt! And it will be all ours!"

"Hee, hee," the taller man laughed. "That'll make us rich!"

The shorter man said, "And we won't tell anybody. We don't want a bunch of people coming here to share in the wealth. We've got to make Sunshine Gap a ghost town, and keep it that way!"

Rosita and Jorge looked at each other wide-eyed. Was it true? Was there copper on their land? They had to tell their father. He couldn't sell this land now! And no one should leave Sunshine Gap! Everybody should share in the wealth!

Rosita whispered to Christina, "They're just about at the creek. It's right behind that rise."

"It won't take them long to dump the poison in the creek!" Christina cried, not wanting to think of the consequences. "We might have to take on those two guys ourselves!"

"What!" Grant almost yelled. "Christina, you're crazy! We're just a bunch of kids!"

"We can still wreak some havoc," Christina replied, "like chase the mule away before they unload the bag of poison! Besides, they're not armed. Just watch out for their shovels."

"Maybe I can whistle for my colt," Jorge said, his imagination running wild. "With Domino running like the wind, I can whip by them, bombing them with rocks!"

"Hurry, Papa! Hurry, police!" Grant exclaimed. "It's getting so scary! If they don't come soon, I'll just want to scream and scram!"

"We may have to scram," Christina agreed, "but not yet!"

The kids watched anxiously as the two men edged closer to the creek. The men continued to talk and laugh. Suddenly, Christina remembered where she heard the taller man's voice. It was in the pizza parlor! He was Dusty, the motorcycle rider!

The shorter man started sneezing, and pulled off his bandana to wipe his nose.

"In the dark it's hard to see," Rosita whispered. "But I think it's Dead Eye!"

"That makes sense," Christina said. "That mule has Dead Eye's brand. And Dusty is the other guy — the one who scared us, the one who thinks he's the ghost of Three Finger McGee!"

"Shall we charge them?" Jorge asked. He was just about to whistle for his colt when he saw the headlights of a vehicle approaching the creek from behind the rise. He said, "Thank heavens! Guys, look! They're here!"

"Good!" Christina said. "Dead Eye and Dusty won't be able to see them coming from that direction."

Rosita's eyes were glued to the two men, who had taken the bag off the mule. "They're cutting the bag open!" she wailed.

"Hurry! Hurry!" Grant yelled. "I can't stand it!"

The two men had just lifted the bag over the side of the creek, when a voice yelled, "Halt! This is the police!"

A swarm of flashlights centered on the two men, who froze like deer caught in the headlights of an oncoming car. Two policemen, along with the sheriff, Big Jim, grabbed the culprits.

"Well, if it ain't Dead Eye and Dusty!" Big Jim said sarcastically, as he put the men in handcuffs. "I suppose you've been 'purifying' the water for the Alonzos, huh?" Big Jim then ordered one of the policemen to take the bag of poison as evidence.

Another van pulled up, carrying Mimi, Papa, and the Alonzos. The adults jumped out of the vehicle, calling out the kids' names.

"Christina!"

"Jorge!"

"Rosita!"

"Grant!"

From out of the dark, Grant yelled in his loudest-ever voice, "We're here!"

The kids charged out into the light of the headlight beams, and hugged their family members. Grant then handed his camera memory chip to the police. It was an important piece of evidence.

"Christina, it appears you were right," Mimi said. "Those two guys were up to no good! The jig is up for those two, and you've solved another mystery."

Mr. Alonzo said, "I hope Dead Eye and Dusty go to the hoosegow for a good long time!"

Rosita grabbed her father's arm. "Dead Eye says there's copper on this land!" she exclaimed. "It's in a vein that's connected to the old Eureka Gulch mine."

"That's why they were poisoning the water," Christina added. "They hoped you would move away or sell the land to them!"

"Does that mean we'll be rich?" Jorge asked.

Mr. Alonzo was speechless for a moment. He wrapped his arms around Rosita and Jorge. "I'm just so glad you're safe and the water wasn't poisoned again!" he exclaimed. "We need to celebrate!"

20 A Rip-Roaring Good Time

The next day, the police determined that the contents of the bag were a form of poison used to mimic toxic runoff from mines. Others in Sunshine Gap were also targeted by the culprits because a copper vein probably ran like tree roots everywhere under the town!

In the evening, everyone gathered at China Betty's to discuss the poisoning of the water, cleaning it up, and finding of copper on their land. People were happy that the problem of the water was solved. It was a bonus that they also might get some extra money. The restaurant was alive with excitement. Every table was filled with local citizens discussing the recent events. Even old Indian Begay was there.

Everyone also wanted to hear the four kids explain how they cracked the mystery of Eureka Gulch.

"We all helped solve the mystery," Christina said. She stood up and motioned to Rosita, Jorge, and Grant, who were sitting at the same table with her. "Rosita provided useful information, Jorge gave good directions, and Grant supplied evidence with his video."

Christina then thanked the old Indian for giving her the warnings of the coyote drawing and the carving, as well as telling her his dream. "That really made me start thinking," Christina said, smiling at Mr. Begay, "especially when I read what coyotes symbolize in the Navajo religion. They are tricksters, warning that something unusual is about to happen." She paused and then asked, "Mr. Begay, why did you choose to show us the coyote images?"

The old Indian smiled and said, "Because I also had a dream that you had come to help us!"

Everyone began chattering about Mr. Begay's dream.

Big Jim stood up. "We all understand that Mr. Begay has a strange way of knowing things," he said. "Kids, please continue with your story."

Christina related the events that led to solving the mystery. Everyone in the restaurant then clapped and cheered for the kids.

"The mystery of the haunted ghost town is solved!" Big Jim announced. "This calls for a real celebration. Before we start the shindig, these smart and brave kids deserve **kudos**. We have tokens of our appreciation to give Rosita, Jorge, Grant, and Christina. China Betty, you do the honors."

China Betty shuffled forward and presented a gift to each of the kids. Jorge's gift was a cowboy hat, Rosita received a silver necklace, Grant got a silver buckle for his belt, and Christina received the bracelet she wanted from the store.

"Wow! Thanks!" the kids whooped in unison as they lifted their gifts up for all to see.

"Thanks to you," Big Jim said, "we and our cattle are now safer, and maybe we are all a little richer!"

Christina smiled and gazed around the room. "These presents are wonderful, but what makes Grant and I most happy is that this town will not become another ghost town. Now, it could become a boom town!"

Big Jim called out, "Let the shindig begin!"

An old man in the corner struck up a strong, vibrant note on the fiddle and the music flowed.

Papa bowed to Christina. "May I have this dance?" he asked. "I'd like to honor our masterful mystery-solver!"

"Of course, Papa," she replied, taking Papa's hand.

"That dance floor still has lots of room on it," Grant remarked, grabbing Mimi's hand and motioning to Jorge and Rosita. "Let's boogie!"

The End

About the Author

Carole Marsh is an author and publisher who has written many works of fiction and non-fiction for young readers. She travels throughout the United States and around the world to research her books. In 1979 Carole Marsh was named Communicator of the Year for her corporate communications work with major national and international corporations.

Marsh is the founder and CEO of Gallopade International, established in 1979. Today, Gallopade International is widely recognized as a leading source of educational materials for every state and many countries. Marsh and Gallopade were recipients of the 2004 Teachers' Choice Award. Marsh has written more than 50 Carole Marsh Mysteries™. In 2007, she was named Georgia Author of the year. Years ago, her children, Michele and Michael, were the original characters in her mystery books. Today, they continue the Carole Marsh Books tradition by working at Gallopade. By adding grandchildren Grant and Christina as new mystery characters, she has continued the tradition for a third generation.

Ms. Marsh welcomes correspondence from her readers. You can e-mail her at fanclub@gallopade.com, visit carolemarshmysteries.com, or write to her in care of Gallopade International, P.O. Box 2779, Peachtree City, Georgia, 30269 USA.

Built-In Book Club
Talk About It!

1. What kind of animal did Christina spot on the ground as the *Mystery Girl* prepared to land in Arizona? Why did it upset her so much? How would you feel if you had witnessed that scene?

2. Big Jim got his nickname because he was such a large person. Do you know anyone with a nickname that describes something about that person? Talk about how nicknames can sometimes be fun and sometimes be hurtful.

3. Christina and Grant were hot while visiting Sunshine Gap. What is the climate like where you live? Is it hot most of the time, or cold most of the time? Which type of weather do you prefer? Why?

4. Christina and Grant learned that ranchers brand cattle to identify them. Can you think of any other ways they might identify their own animals besides branding?

5. What was your favorite part of the story? Why?

6. Eureka Gulch felt spooky to the kids. Have you ever seen an abandoned house or even an abandoned office building? Did it seem spooky to you? Why or why not?

7. Have you ever been on a camping trip? If so, what did you like about it and what did you dislike about it?

8. In this mystery, Christina used her cell phone to call for help, and Grant used his digital camera to video the bad guys. Do you have similar high-tech devices in your home? How do you use them?

9. Which character did you like best in the mystery? Why?

10. Jorge was upset because his colt got sick. How can you help someone when they are sad?

Built-In Book Club

Bring It to Life!

1. Create your own tombstones! Christina and Grant read some clever inscriptions on the tombstones at Boot Hill. Gather art supplies and poster board and create some tremendous tombstones! Cut your tombstones out of the poster board and glue stands to the back of them. Set them around your book club meeting and take a tour of your own spooky graveyard!

2. Find out about mines! Mines are very dangerous places to work, but mining is a very important industry. Divide your book club into groups. Use the Internet to determine some natural resources that are found in mines. Assign several natural resources to each group. Then, ask each group to research their natural resources and list the

products made from those natural resources. You will probably be amazed at what can be found deep in the ground!

3. Brand it! Back in the old days, there were no fences on the western prairie. Cattle roamed on an "open range." Brands were used to identify cattle from different ranches. Create your own brand, using letters from your name. Draw it on a piece of poster board. Then, name it...and claim it!

4. Map it out! Bring in a large map of the United States. Find your town and your state. Find Tombstone, Arizona. List all the states you would have to travel through to get from your home state to Arizona. If you have a mileage key on your map, figure out how many miles you would have to travel!

Glossary

ambush: to attack by surprise

artifact: an object made and used by human beings who lived a long time ago

artifice: a clever trick or crafty device

constrain: to restrain or confine

covert: secret; disguised

desolate: barren; dreary; gloomy

flaccid: soft and limp; not strong

foray: an initial attempt, or a sudden, short attack

hoosegow: a jail

kudos: praise; flattering comments

sinister: threatening, or foreshadowing evil

skedaddle: to run away quickly

trespass: to enter another's property without permission

vittles: food

Scavenger Hunt

Want to have some fun? Let's go on a scavenger hunt! See if you can find the items below related to the mystery. *(Teachers: you have permission to reproduce this page.)*

_____ 1. a cowboy hat

_____ 2. a flashlight

_____ 3. a picture of a cactus plant

_____ 4. a white foam coffee cup

_____ 5. a paper plate

_____ 6. a pocketknife
      (for carving, like Mr. Begay!)

_____ 7. a cell phone

_____ 8. a piece of pizza

_____ 9. a sleeping bag (for camping!)

_____ 10. a silver belt buckle

Pop Quiz

1. What was the name of the restaurant where Christina, Grant, Mimi, and Papa ate "vittles" when they first arrived in Sunshine Gap?

2. What was the name of Rosita and Jorge's father?

3. What animal was drawn on the back of Papa's rented SUV?

4. What does RIP mean?

5. True or False? A tarantula crawled out from under a paper plate onto Christina's sleeve.

6. Why were the stars so bright out in the desert?

7. What attacked Grant and Christina in the mineshaft?

8. How many fingers did Dusty have on his right hand?

Tombstone and Arizona Trivia

1. Tombstone founder Edward Schieffelin discovered silver in the area in 1877. Silver and gold mining was big business over the next seven years until rising underground water forced a stop to mining operations.

2. By 1863, one in every four people in Arizona was a miner.

3. The famous gunfight at the OK Corral was an example of the lawlessness that marked Tombstone in the late 1800s. President Chester Arthur even threatened to send in military troops to restore order!

4. Tombstone's nickname is "The Town Too Tough to Die!"

5. Tombstone supplied manganese to the government during World War I, and lead during World War II.

6. In 1884, the Boot Hill Graveyard was declared to be full and officially closed to burials.

7. On September 30, 1962, Tombstone was named a National Historic Landmark.

8. Arizona has more than 100 ghost towns, including Bumble Bee, Gunsight, Ruby, Copper Creek, Crown King, Fort Misery, and Jerome.

9. Arizona leads the nation in copper production. Copper is used in wiring and in coins, like pennies!

10. A saguaro cactus grows arms only after it is about 15 feet tall and about 75 years old! The biggest saguaro cacti are about 200 years old.

11. The town of Bisbee is known as the "Queen of the Copper Mines."

Enjoy this exciting excerpt from

THE MYSTERY IN LAS VEGAS

1 TIGER TRICKS

As an eerie green glow began to illuminate the stage, Christina watched a ghostly white fog roll toward her. The soft music was growing louder. Christina could not only hear it, she could feel it rumbling in her chest.

Suddenly, ice-blue eyes pierced the mist like blazing sapphires, burning a path for two slinking tigers. Completely white except for their black stripes, they looked more phantom than feline. Christina's younger brother, Grant, yelped. "You pinched my arm!"

"Owww!"

"Sorry," Christina mumbled, "I thought it was the chair's arm!" She brushed her long brown hair over her shoulders and settled back into her seat.

Christina knew this was only a rehearsal for the Mysteries Hotel Magic Show, but she couldn't help gripping the arms of her front-row seat in the darkness. This was her first trip to Las Vegas and it was exciting!

The owner of the hotel, Mr. Jenkins, was a friend of Christina and Grant's grandfather, Papa. Mr. Jenkins invited them to see the magic show rehearsal the minute they arrived at the hotel. They hadn't even been to their rooms yet!

Christina jumped as a booming voice announced, "Rescued from the jungles of India, they've come to share their magic with you! Ladies and gentlemen, meet the world's most regal and rare twins—Soman and Shiba!"

"Those are the most beautiful creatures I've ever seen," Christina said.

Grant's jaw dropped open as he watched the stage through binoculars. "W-w-wow," he stuttered.

"My turn," declared Mimi, the children's grandmother, peeking through Grant's binoculars.

"Oh, my," she added, "they are just magnificent!"

"Look!" Grant whispered to Christina, as a girl and boy entered from each side of the stage to meet the tigers. "They're just kids!"

Spotlights focused on two large, mirrored, rotating globes that shot spears of pink light into the dark auditorium. The boy and girl commanded Soman and Shiba to jump onto the globes.

"And now," the announcer continued, "the only one these royal tigers bow to—the Maharaja of Magic, Manendra!"

Out walked a man in a sparkling blue costume and jeweled turban. Soman and Shiba changed from calm tigers to hissing, swatting beasts as he approached.

Manendra thrust his hands into the air and the fog crept back across the stage. Christina noticed two silver rings floating from the ceiling toward each of the tigers.

"I don't see any wires!" Grant exclaimed. "Do you see wires, Christina?"

As the rings neared the tigers, the music grew louder and a puff of silver smoke shot out of the globes where the tigers sat. The music stopped suddenly and the rings hit the floor with a thud. The tigers were gone!

"How'd they do that?" Grant said, clapping.

"Magic," Mimi answered.

When the music started again, Christina saw something else descending from the ceiling. It was the tigers! They had reappeared and were being lowered to the stage on small circular platforms.

"Come and bow!" the magician commanded. The tigers left their platforms obediently and bowed to Manendra. He patted each on the head and motioned for them to leave the stage.

Christina noticed the tigers were once again very calm. She expected the boy and girl to escort the tigers away, but two men who were not in costumes led them offstage.

"Give me those binoculars!" Christina ordered, before Grant had time to take them off his neck.

"You're choking me!" Grant exclaimed.

"Oh! Sorry, Grant," Christina said.

It was hard to tell with the stage lighting, but as Christina took a closer look at the tigers, they looked different. She had the feeling something wasn't right!

2 TRACKING THE TEARS

"So, what did you think, kids?" Mr. Jenkins asked, as soon as the house lights came on.

"It was awesome!" was Grant's quick reply.

Despite her strange feeling that something was wrong, Christina agreed. "Mr. Jenkins, everyone will want to see Soman and Shiba!"

"I know you folks are tired and ready to get to bed," Mr. Jenkins observed. "Your luggage and room keys are at the check-in desk. I'll see you at breakfast tomorrow morning."

Walking from the hotel theater to the desk was a new experience for Grant and Christina. Following a red, tiled path, they moved into a huge room as dark and cool as a cave. On each side, coins clattered, bells clanged and lights flashed. The constant hum of people talking was occasionally interrupted by joyous screams.

"What is this place?" Grant asked, his blue eyes opened wide. "I've never seen so much bling-bling! And it's so loud in here!"

"This is the hotel casino," Mimi said. "Almost every hotel in Las Vegas has one." She slung her beaded red shawl over her shoulders. "I'm too tired to explain tonight. I'll tell you all about it later, OK?"

"Yep, little doggies," said Papa, looking tall and rugged in his black cowboy hat and chocolate-brown leather boots. "It's time to hit the sack!"

Christina knew how Mimi felt. She had felt like she was coming down with a cold since they left their home in Georgia. But Christina didn't want anyone to know she didn't feel well. She and Grant had worked too hard to be included on this trip.

Christina and Grant often traveled with Mimi and Papa. Mimi wrote mysteries for children, and often traveled to do research for her books. But this trip to visit Papa's old friend, Mr. Jenkins, and one of the country's largest air shows, Aviation Nation, at Nellis Air Force Base near Las Vegas, was a different story. Mimi had to be convinced it was a good idea!

Christina remembered the conversation almost word for word.

"Las Vegas is not a place for kids," Mimi had said.

"But, Mimi," Christina had replied, "it's not an adults-only town like it was when you were a kid. Now, there are roller coasters, chocolate factories, magic shows and lots of other things kids love. It's educational, too. We can even visit King Tut's tomb!"

Grant had also done his homework. "Did you know there are hotels in Las Vegas that look like New York, Paris and lots of other places?" he had piped in. "It's like every place in one place!"

Impressed by all the things the kids had learned, Mimi finally declared defeat. "You win!" she had told them. "Besides, a hotel called 'Mysteries' is the perfect place for a family of mystery solvers to visit," she added, referring to the kids' uncanny ability to get mixed up in a mystery wherever they traveled!

Grant and Christina dragged their luggage into the suite they were sharing with Mimi and Papa. Grant immediately started making footprints in the freshly vacuumed carpet.

"Do you think Clue could follow this trail?" he asked, thinking of their dog they had left at home.

Christina shuffled into the bathroom to brush her teeth. When she stopped to rinse, she heard a strange noise on the other side of the wall. The way it was echoing, she guessed it was coming from the stairwell next to their room.

"Did you hear that, Grant?" she asked her brother, who was now drawing tic-tac-toe shapes in the carpet.

"Hear what?" he asked, annoyed with the interruption.

"Come in here!" Christina said.

"It sounds like someone is crying," Grant observed. "I wonder what's wrong. Do you think someone fell down the stairs?"

"I didn't think of that!" Christina said. "We'd better go and see if they're OK." Christina grabbed their room card-key and they rushed to the stairwell.

A girl about Christina's age sat near the top of the stairs. Long ebony hair fell around her face like a black waterfall, almost touching the stairs as she rested her head on her knees. She wore a sparkling, ice-blue outfit.

"Are you all right?" Christina asked.

"Did you fall down the stairs?" Grant added.

"No, I didn't fall," the girl answered, lifting her head. Mournful brown eyes peered up at them. Her thick accent was a clue that she was probably not from Las Vegas.

"Did my crying wake you?" she asked.

"We weren't in bed yet," Christina answered. "We just got here."

"Why are you crying?" Grant asked, tired of chit-chat and wanting to get to the point.

The TRAIL of '98

DAWSON CITY

YUKON TERRITORY

UNITED STATES
CANADA

YUKON RIVER

CHILKOOT PASS · TAGISH LAKE

DYEA · WHITE PASS
SKAGWAY

BRITISH COLUMBIA

ALASKA TERRITORY

JUNEAU

CANADA
UNITED STATES

GULF OF ALASKA

TO SEATTLE

Enjoy this exciting excerpt from

THE "GOSH AWFUL" GOLD RUSH MYSTERY

1 THE GOLD DOME

Christina was convinced that this was going to be one of the most fun adventures that she had ever been on with her grandmother, Mimi, her grandfather, Papa, little brother, Grant, and a couple of friends that they were picking up to join them on the trip.

At the moment, they were standing around the *Mystery Girl*, Papa's little red and white airplane, on the tarmac at a small airport near Dahlonega, Georgia. Mimi, who spent most of her time writing kid's mystery books, was investigating a very curious mystery of her own. She had inherited—from a total stranger—a gold mine!

"I'm sure that if we make a quick stop in Dahlonega, I can find out something about the Gold Bug," Mimi said. She was eager to get underway. The Gold Bug was the name of the mine she had inherited. She believed that the Gold Rush museum in Dahlonega might have some information on it. She had to start somewhere. The will had not said where the Gold Bug was located.

"How about a little lunch, first?" pleaded Papa. He was always ready for a bowl of soup at lunchtime, and could always entice Mimi with a promise of unsweetened ice tea with lemon and lots of ice—her favorite.

Christina watched Mimi sway her blond curls back and forth as she thought. She tapped the toe of one of her red high heels. No one hoped more than her grandkids that she would give in—they were starving!

Leg 1: Peachtree City to Dahlonega

They'd gotten a pre-dawn start at Falcon Field in Peachtree City, Georgia. As soon as they'd taken off over the pine forests, Papa warned them to "Watch closely!"

They couldn't imagine what kind of surprise he could have for them this early in the morning up in the dark sky. But in just a moment, the sun broke over the horizon. As they banked left to circle past the city of Atlanta, sunlight struck the dome of the state capitol building. It glistened so vividly, that they had to hide their eyes behind their hands.

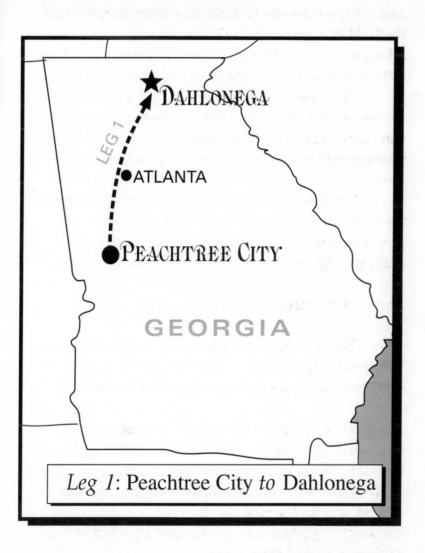

Leg 1: Peachtree City *to* Dahlonega

"You know where all that gold on the dome of the Georgia capitol building came from?" asked Papa.

When the kids yawned and said, "No," he reminded them, "That gold came from a gold rush in our very own state in Dahlonega!"

Mimi looked at the gold watch on her arm, hidden beneath the sleeve of her red suit jacket. "Where we'll be shortly?" she asked hopefully.

"Sooner than those poor folks," said Papa, pointing down to the interstate highway far beneath them, clogged with cars stuck in the morning rush hour.

Grant and Christina yawned again. "Think I'll get in a little nap," said Grant, tugging his jacket up over his shoulders.

But almost before he could nod off, he heard Papa talking to the controllers at the small airport where they were to land. And with one small bounce, they were down, and the adventure had begun.

And, as usual, a mysterious adventure it would be!

2 THE "FIRST" OF MANY GOLD RUSHES

Regarding lunch, Mimi nodded, and Papa led them to a cute café on the quaint town square of Dahlonega, Georgia. The square was busy this sunny Saturday afternoon. The bustling café looked like a giant indoor picnic was in progress with its white tables, checkered tablecloths, yellow daisies in white vases, and families eating and chatting.

They picked a table by the window and ordered homemade pimiento cheese and egg salad sandwiches, chili made with buffalo for Papa, iced tea for Mimi, and big, fat Snickerdoodle cookies for Christina and Grant.

As they waited for the waitress to bring their food, Papa said, "So tell us what you discovered at the museum this morning, and we'll tell you what we bought in a local shop." He gave the kids a wink and they giggled. Clearly, a secret was afoot!

"Yes, Mimi," said Christina, "Tell us again how you came to be the proud new owner of a gold mine!"

Mimi laughed. "It's like I told you," she said, sipping her tea, which had a bright green sprig of mint on top, "a lawyer called me. She said that she was handling the will of a Mr. Jamison Lynn who had died recently of natural causes. He was 104!"

"Wow!" interrupted Grant, "That's older than dirt!"

"Depends on how old the dirt is, buddy," Papa reminded him.

"Let Mimi talk," pleaded Christina. "We want to hear this story."

Mimi smiled at her granddaughter. Christina loved stories—she liked to read them and write them and tell them. "Well, apparently, Mr. Lynn left me the only thing he still owned at the time of his death—a gold mine named the Gold Bug."

Now it was Christina who interrupted. "I've read a story by that name by Edgar Allan Poe. It was really cool; a little scary, but an exciting mystery."

"I always loved that story, too," Mimi agreed. "Edgar Allan Poe was one of my favorites when I was a teenager."

"Excuse us!" said Grant, with a look to his sister. "Back to Mimi's story, please."

"Ok, ok," Mimi said, as the waitress set down their yummy-looking lunches. "The lawyer said that there was little information about the Gold Bug, except that it's somewhere in Alaska."

Papa roared so loud with laughter that the cowboy hat he always wore tipped back on his head. "That helps a whole lot! Somewhere in Alaska, a state made up of a gazillion square miles, most of it frozen!"

"We could get lucky," Christina said with a frown. She really believed that they would find the Gold Bug.

Her grandfather just laughed some more. "That would be a LOT of luck," he said. "You know, depending on luck is how so many folks went bust back during the days of the Gold Rush."

Grant patiently picked the pimiento out of his pimiento cheese. "I'm confused," he said. "If Mr. Lynn was from Georgia, like you told us, then how did he end up owning a gold mine in faraway Alaska?"

"Oh, Grant," said Mimi, "you have to understand more about the Gold Rush." She got a dreamy look in her eyes and they all knew that they were in for a short lecture.

"The Gold Rush was more than just an event, it was a dream, a state of mind," Mimi continued. "Most people lived hard, poor, rough and tumble lives back in the 1800s. They wanted desperately to improve their lives. So when word got out that gold had been discovered in California, it set into motion an amazing chapter of American history!"

"But all that was in California," said Grant. "I still don't understand the Georgia connection."

"Gold's not just found in California," Mimi explained. "There was gold found in Georgia, North Carolina, and other places. Georgia claims the so-called 'first' Gold Rush. But it was California where gold fever struck. People from all over the eastern part of the United States packed up and headed west to seek their fortune, all the way up to Alaska."

Suddenly, Grant got a sort of "gold fever" look in his eyes. "You mean I might find gold right here in Georgia if I dug for it?"

Mimi smiled. "Just maybe," she said. "There are places you can pan for gold around here."

"You might as well buy a lottery ticket," warned Papa, who was a lot bigger on working hard than he was on gambling or waiting for "Lady Luck" to help you out.

But Christina understood that her grandfather was just setting up their surprise. "But you *could* find gold here in Dahlonega, couldn't you, Papa?" she asked with a grin.

Papa grinned back. "Oh, I'm certain that all that glitters is indeed gold here in Dahlonega."

Mimi was suspicious. She looked at Grant, but he just pretended to zip his mouth closed. There was certainly a mystery at their table—and Mimi was the one who was in the dark!

WRITE YOUR OWN MYSTERY!

Make up a dramatic title!

You can pick four real kid characters!

Select a real place for the story's setting!

Try writing your first draft!

Edit your first draft!

Read your final draft aloud!

You can add art, photos or illustrations!

Share your book with others and send me a copy!

Six Secret Writing Tips from Carole Marsh!

WOULD YOU **CAROLE MARSH MYSTERIES** LIKE TO BE
A CHARACTER IN A CAROLE MARSH MYSTERY?

If you would like to star in a Carole Marsh Mystery, fill out the form below and write a 25-word paragraph about why you think you would make a good character! Once you're done, ask your mom or dad to send this page to:

Carole Marsh Mysteries Fan Club
Gallopade International
P.O. Box 2779
Peachtree City, GA 30269

My name is: _____

I am a: ____ boy ____ girl   Age: _____

I live at: _____

City: _____   State: ____   Zip code: _____

My e-mail address: _____

My phone number is: _____

_____

_____

_____

_____

_____

_____

_____

_____

_____

_____

VISIT THE CAROLE MARSH MYSTERIES WEBSITE

www.carolemarshmysteries.com

- *Check out what's coming up next! Are we coming to your area with our next book release? Maybe you can have your book signed by the author!*

- *Join the Carole Marsh Mysteries Fan Club!*

- *Apply for the chance to be a character in an upcoming Carole Marsh Mystery!*

- *Learn how to write your own mystery!*